T0277868

General Firebrand and His Red Atlas

THE INDIA LIST

GENERAL
FIREBRAND
AND HIS
RED ATLAS

Tathagata Bhattacharya

LONDON CALCUTTA NEW YORK

Seagull Books, 2024

© Tathagata Bhattacharya, 2024

First published by Seagull Books, 2024

ISBN 978 1 80309 357 4

British Library Cataloguing-in-Publication Data

A catalogue record for this book is available from the British Library

Typeset by Seagull Books, Calcutta, India

Printed and bound by WordsWorth India, New Delhi, India

To

my mother, Pranati Chaudhuri (Bhattacharya),
my father, Nabarun Bhattacharya,
my grandfather, Bijon Bhattacharya,
and my grandmother, Mahasweta Devi

Acknowledgements

The acknowledgement section of any book is usually about gratitude and thankfulness. But should that really be all? I would like to begin my acknowledgements by first acknowledging the power of words.

What ought to be the words of a novel like? What colour should those words wear? Are the words well-fed? Did they have their mothers around them when their fates were being sealed after many days of starvation? Are they sane after being without medicines or electricity for more than two months? Many have been truncated into mangled bits and pieces as the bombs hit them in Gaza. Many words of children were melted to make soap for the German SS officers in Buchenwald and Belsen. Many words have been beheaded, some firebombed.

Some words are like guerrillas, they are always going to escape. They will go here and there. You cannot gauge their trajectory of travel, and they will always return fire. Some words are dead. They have been buried far and deep inside the forests. Some words have been raped and then burnt to ash. Words are crazy—they are cruel, they are unpredictable. In my short life, I have known many such words. These words move me. Words of safety have never interested me.

But words are also forever. Manuscripts don't burn, no matter how much fuel you put into the fire. Even words forged in fear today can become the words of someone's courage tomorrow. A small part of my father's 'Poem on Vietnam' comes to mind: A false poem can contain more lies than an American President spews out on a routine basis / But a true poem protects children from bombing raids throughout the night.' The translation is mine, from Bengali to English.

I want to acknowledge that words for me are never going to be a collection of alphabets—they are ingredients of fire and possible arson, hopefully on a large scale, on a very, very large scale, of revolt against injustice. Because we have forgotten that the weak and the meek also have a right to exist, as do animals and insects, birds and bees, trees and forests, mountains and rivers.

I want to acknowledge my beloved parents, Nabarun Bhattacharya and Pranati Bhattacharya, and my grandparents Bijon Bhattacharya and Mahasweta Devi. I owe them all an immeasurable debt of gratitude for introducing me to a world rich in literature, theatre, cinema, art, strong politics and audacious thought. A world in which one never sat on the fence. They taught me to cultivate a spine, to speak up and stand strong against injustice, even if it might seem strange to society, to be empathetic to animals and trees, to the soil and its insects. Their lessons have shaped not only this novel but also my very being. Their deeds will be hard to measure up to, but then, they also taught me not to worry about comparisons and rat races.

How can I not mention my wife, Nilanjana Bhowmick, who has pushed me indefatigably? She has believed in me, even when I didn't. I never believed I could write a book. My parents and my grandmother did—and Nila did too (In fact, Nila possibly believes that I can scale Mount Godwin Austen even at this age and come back alive.) And she does so in spite of her rigorous writing schedule as an author and a journalist, day in and day out.

And then there are my children—Che, Kuttush and Gypsy. Uff! What a lively little bunch they are. Always keeping me on my feet. Che, the human child, our budding psychologist, has been always on hand with his analyses and his Gen Z iterations: 'You will be OK, Bau!' And Gypsy and Kuttush, every time I seem to have run out of ideas, one of them who comes running to me with a toy clenched in his or her mouth.

I am grateful to some dear friends who sent me their opinion in the formative stage of the work: Jeff, Kathakoli, Turbashu, Jamie, Shaon, Daliya. Thanks for taking time out of your busy schedules.

This book's journey has also been shaped by the support and encouragement of Naveen Kishore and Sunandini Banerjee at Seagull Books. Their belief in this book and in me has been a source of immense strength. I am deeply grateful for their guidance and their faith in me.

And finally, to you, the readers, I entrust the fate of this novel. *General Firebrand and His Red Atlas* is a coming together of many fears—personal, political, past, present and future.

It's in your hands now.

Over and out,
Tathagata.

I

The night the great long-horned bird impaled itself on the metal fangs of the giant watchtower overlooking the old jetty at Devil's Lair, events began to unfold at breakneck speed in the self-proclaimed independent realm of Sands.

About 12 walking hours away, Colonel Firebrand was with his battalion of night-watch volunteers. The team had kept vigil for 11 nights, and spent long hours without sleep. He relieved the unit, explained the return-patrol path and then watched them as they disappeared into the distance.

He had chosen the spot well. He was good with things like that. That is why the People's Resistance Committee, or PRC according to the Tantilash newspapers, had entrusted him with this sector in the first place. It was the last field where the paddy had risen to its rightful height. Just a few more weeks and the slaughter would begin, the sickles cutting the stalks down to size. Then Firebrand would have to find new positions for the sand gunnies. For now, it was the best tactical position from which to defend Sands against any western onslaught. Flanked by crocodile creeks, the 3-kilometre-wide grazing field could easily be covered by 800 riflemen and 60 machine gunners on a reasonably moonlit night like this.

'Spread out, and then catch your bones. No coupling, no bungling—got that, newbies?' he growled at the new battalion as he slumped to the ground. He took off his tight boots and wiggled his toes. At 55, he was the oldest of the lot, and he was beginning to feel it. He began to massage his ankles, his fingernails occasionally gnawing at the rock-hard fossil of a corn on the little toe of his right foot. And then, stretching out, he reached into his trouser pocket and, with practised precision, brought out a black-metal cigarette case.

Inherited from his father, it had a flag of Yugoslavia on one side and an engraving on the other that could no longer be read due to the massive wear and tear it had endured. Firebrand's boys and girls had never heard of Yugoslavia. Only Aks had, but then Aks usually knew a little something about everything under the sun. Firebrand liked Aks a lot.

Firebrand lit one of his carefully rationed hand-rolled cigarettes and took a few deep puffs. By the searchlight of the moon, the sky looked like a giant black canvas riddled with gunshot stars. As the nicotine soothed his nerves, his mind began to flicker. He thought about the son he'd last seen 14 years ago. He was away, so far away, in the bustling City of No Sleep with his mother. How was she? How was his son? What was he doing in the City of No Sleep, home to 30 million people?

He could almost hear Ryan telling the story of the boy, the old man and the giant fish. He could see his little hands mimic the movements of the oar, the grab at the water . . . When, suddenly, a voice as loud as thunder roared in his ear:

'Motherfucker, in the middle of a war and pissing tears for your family? Stalin would have sent you to the Gulag!'

Firebrand sat up with a start and turned to locate the voice. It seemed to be coming from behind him. Gun in hand, he turned over on his belly and began to crawl in that direction.

'Ten o'clock, soldier,' the voice boomed again.

Firebrand sidled over a little to the left and kept crawling. But he was scared. Something told him that the AK-74 in his hand was not going to be much use. It had been a voice like no other, as if from a different world, from a man who breathed a different air. Firebrand had heard Sir John Gielgud's narration of Saki's stories as a child, sitting next to his father. He suddenly remembered those evenings. If Gielgud's was the limit of the human baritone, this was certainly a phantom call.

He kept moving, his bare toes taking occasional snips at the strands of the harvest. And just as his head was about to ram into a bamboo pole, he stopped and looked up. A scarecrow was perched on top. A scarecrow that then began to speak.

'Listen, son. What I'm about to tell you is of the greatest importance. You lot have done a commendable job thus far. But now the game's going to get much bigger. We need to prepare and we need to prepare well. You understand me, yes?'

Firebrand was cold with fear. In the world that he came from, scarecrows did not speak.

'Who are you?' he whispered.

'Konstantin Rokossovsky.'

Every inkling that one of his team was playing a prank on him was wiped clean out of his mind. None of them could be remotely aware of Marshal Rokossovsky.

'Pay attention!' the Marshal continued, oblivious to Firebrand's dazed expression. 'There will be many more joining the party. It will be something the world has never seen before.'

'You're a ghost!'

'Yes and no. I am the past. When the present ignores the past and slides swiftly downhill, the past is compelled to send a reminder. History repeats itself when the past is forgotten, son. There will be time enough for us to talk of philosophy and politics and history, the rains on the steppe, even Stalin's megalomania. But not now. Now I must go. Our next communication will be in its own time. Maybe a week from now. Maybe a month. I leave you with two important tasks. Every able-bodied man and woman in Sands must have digging tools. Spades, shovels, mattocks, whatever.'

'What for?'

'This is the problem with guerrilla forces and too much democratization. In war, you follow the orders of your superior officer, son. And you can trust my words—I've seen some serious shit in my time.'

'I know, Marshal. I read your memoirs when I was 14. Kursk, Stalingrad, Dubno, Moscow, Operation Bagration. I was fascinated by your accounts.'

'Oh, they translated it into English too, eh? All right. Now, the second important task is to identify high grounds in Sands.

Sixty metres above sea level, especially at the dockyard. Enough to shelter the entire population. Some areas need to be covered, for the children, the sick, the old and the livestock. Permanent concrete structures will be best. Grains and essential belongings must be stored and covered with waterproof sheets. You'll need lighters, ropes, candles, matchboxes, weapons and ammo, twine, tarpaulin, medicines—a year's supply, at the least. I'm afraid you don't have much time. You have the next month and a half to get this done. Oh yes, also strong iron poles, 20 metres long, enough in number to cover the perimeter of Sands at a distance of 5 metres from each other. 10 metres into the earth, 10 metres out in the open. Holes drilled into them, large ones, at a height of 1 metre from the ground. And don't forget the strong rope, hundreds of miles of it.'

Firebrand was already thinking: How the hell do I explain this to the PRC? Even if they believe me, where will the money come from?

'Invoke the powers vested in you by the PRC and convene a meeting of the military council at Kalponik Theatre. Make sure the window on the western side is kept open. The rest will be taken care of. Over and out, Colonel.'

The next morning, the residents climbed up to the watchtower and brought down the dead bird. Built a pyre and cremated it, and spread its ashes on the waters of the river that flowed through their town.

II

The announcement of the Lynch Games by Madame President Nida Dodi was a tried-and-tested diversionary tactic, lifted straight out of the administrative textbook of imperial Rome. But this time the wealthy residents of Tantilash were not so easily diverted. Usually, the most expensive tickets—to watch the National Stadium grounds stained red with the blood of anti-nationals—would run out within hours of such announcements. Not so now, and barely a handful of citizen applications volunteering for the lynch mob trickled in.

The Republican Armed Forces and officials were in silent agreement with their fellow men. They did not think this was the best time for sport, not when the government was facing a full-blown civil war, not when millions of people were fighting the Army and the Paramilitary Forces on the ground in the East. The toll on the Republican Army had been particularly heavy this last year, and a steady number of coffins had been coming home to various towns and villages with alarming regularity.

The PRC Guerrillas had cut off the chicken-neck corridor earlier in May, blocking land access to the remote Seven Hills province. The only way of maintaining control was by flying in supplies and troops. But flying out coal and minerals had been an expensive proposition, and the industrialists' lobby and multinational companies had already submitted multiple memoranda with their pleas and complaints to Madame President. Nida Dodi had lent a patient hearing to the industry bodies and chambers of commerce and promised to set her house in order as fast as possible. The delegation had left her office happy and relieved. She was a no-nonsense woman. If she said it, she meant it. She had suspended all welfare schemes and subsidies, hadn't she? The queen of free-market advocacy, she believed in the survival of the fittest, or in the culling of the weak. So three years ago, when the farmers in Trior to the west refused to part with the little stock of grain they had left after two successive years of drought, she refused to raise the government's procurement price. Instead, she gave the farmers a deadline to comply with the government's orders, or else. The farmers were not only ignorant but stubborn too. When the police arrived to seize their stock, they opted for violence. About 77 farmers and 118 policemen lost their lives that day. The farmers set fire to a few police vehicles and stations. They looted some arms and ammunition. And typical of the weak and the poor, they celebrated their victory that night by drinking till they keeled over asleep in their chairs and on their tables.

That night, thousands and thousands of paramilitary troops and provincial constabulary men descended upon Trior. People were pulled out of their beds and shot, stabbed, sliced open or kicked to death. The count of bodies, they say, ran into many thousands, even though Republic Times made no mention of it in their headlines the next morning. The killing continued well into the wee hours. The grains were taken, the women raped.

The government sent in special trains to transport the grains to its warehouses.

Madame President was a woman of her word. If she said it, she meant it. Stories of her childhood had become legend in the Republic. When she was 10, she had swum across a 200-metre-wide river in spate and saved a calf from being washed away. On her way back, she had warded off a crocodile attack. Since she was seven, she'd helped her father run his small tea shop at a bus terminus. She'd wash the dishes and go from one bus window to the next, selling packets of snacks tucked into a basket she carried on her head. At 13, she beat up four men in a forest who were trying to force themselves upon a woman. At 18, she was married off by her father to a man twice her age. But she ran away that very night without consummating the arrangement, and sought refuge in a monastery. There, she received lessons in ideology from the monks and nuns, and was eventually sent to the religious-cultural-nationalist mother organization for paramilitary training. Alongside, she slowly grew convinced about the supremacy of her faith over all others.

Nobody knew how true these stories were, but many believed them fervently. Short animation films were aired on TV about her exploits. Free pamphlets were distributed in city squares, narrating tales of her bravery. School textbooks had chapters on her life of struggle and eventual success.

Thus rose the far-right religious-party leader who swept through the elections in a frenzy, promising every country-man the recovery of all ill-gotten wealth from the politician-bureaucrat-corporate axis of evil and its redistribution among the poor. Promising to turn the Republic into a land of milk and honey, its streets paved with gold. It is a different matter that after coming to power, contrary to those promises, she dedicated her government to enabling the corporate takeover of nearly every inch of land and everything on it and under it. Elections were held once more, but since all the opposition leaders were dead or underground or in jail, Dodi's Heritage Party won them unopposed.

But the defection of more than 60,000 soldiers from the Lightning Strike Corps with materials and warfighting machinery to the PRC had irked the Army. Even the otherwise unfazed Dodi was worried. That was followed by the crossing over of an entire air-defence brigade. The Republican Air Force (RAF) was seriously unnerved. The air chief had faced a near mutiny after 87 of his young aviators were shot down over two weeks.

Still, they had to fly. If coal and minerals did not arrive, it would spell the end of Madame President and her officials, the companies, the armed forces. The glitz of Tantilash and Davnagar would vanish into thin air. The Republic would cease to exist. And that was simply not an option.

III

El Comandante sat flummoxed in his hotel-turned-operational headquarters in Dhamachapa town, towards the north of Sands, in the foothills of the Himalayas. Firebrand had just finished speaking and was now loudly slurping his coffee. El Comandante had known his Colonel for well over 30 years. Firebrand had been his senior in university, and they'd even spent a year together in jail. Their daring escape story was another of Sands' legends. Firebrand's animated explanation to the revolutionary inmates about the application of Gramsci's praxis to the people's struggle against the Republic, his lectures rejecting localized and micro-contextualized struggles for the environment and gender . . . The words still rang in his ears. A lot of the Central Committee members had cut their teeth on Firebrand's tutorials.

'FB, I know it's been tough and none of us are getting any younger. Maybe you should take a break. You know, I think you should meet Dr Kaplan once. He's old now but still sits in that dispensary attached to the mosque on Armenian Church Road, you remember?'

'Kapo, I am not crazy, OK? It'll take me less than a minute to disable the four lads who guard you. Do not fuck with me.'

'FB, remember whom you're speaking to.'

'Yeah, yeah. I've known you since these assholes were in their nappies, Kapo. I could have been anywhere, in any position I chose. It's just that I am a man of action and not wily machinations.'

'I know your actions all too well, FB. Dangling from the balcony in front of Laila and Ryan. Shattering the glass door with your bare feet. You bled litres . . . Couldn't even keep your house in order. You were married more to the bottle, you ass.'

Firebrand slid across the table in a flash and slammed, feet-first, into El Comandante's face. Their bodies crashed to the floor and they grappled and grunted like animals until the door was flung open and the bodyguards rushed in. Yusuf and Rahul, old hands, scrambled to pull Firebrand away while the two others, newcomers, helped up a bleeding Kapo.

El Comandante wiped away the blood with a soiled towel off the table. 'I must say, FB, even at this age, you're as fast as a wolf. It's OK, Yusuf. Take your men out. When two real men meet, blood often flows.'

The guards left, the two new ones trying to hide their surprise. Nobody touched El Comandante and got away with it. They'd seen Brigadiers sent to the firing line for calling El Comandante the son of a whore. So all those tales about Comrade Firebrand must be true.

Yusuf stopped at the door for a moment. 'Will you boys grow up? Real men, my foot. Even on my deathbed, I'll be breaking up your fights.'

Kapo and Firebrand grinned at him shamelessly.

'Now pour me a rum, Kapo,' Firebrand said, as Yusuf shut the door behind him.

'No, FB, you know I won't.'

'For old time's sake, man. I know you have a bottle hidden somewhere.'

'I can't do that, FB.'

'Just one drink, come on. It'll help heal your cut.'

'I'm scared of drinking with you, man.'

Firebrand stood up. 'Kapo, convene the meeting, or I will. Remember, it takes more than bullets to stop an armoured attack. Send us more anti-tank weapons and RPGs. You sit on this chair because I hold entire brigades down. Never forget that.'

Firebrand put out his cigarette on Kapo's table and dropped the stub in his glass of water. Then he put on his battered black trench coat and stomped out of the room and into the rain.

El Comandante sat staring at the door for quite some time. Then he went to the betel-juice-stained wash basin and carefully rinsed his glass to remove every trace of Firebrand's cigarette. Then he poured himself a rum, filled his pipe and opened the window. A cold wind from the Himalayan heights blew in the rain. He could feel it on his face. He lit his pipe and took a sip of the rum. And he saw Firebrand disappear around the corner.

'Obviously, I can't tell them that a scarecrow's asked for a military-council meeting to be convened,' he said aloud, even though the room was empty. He remembered what a jolly man Firebrand used to be, the life of every party at university, always cracking jokes, and that disarming laugh that had such a magnetic effect on the students. He felt a pang of remorse for reminding FB of the old days, of his drinking episodes, of Laila and Ryan.

Kapo had often wondered what his feelings really were for FB. Was it gratitude for saving his life or for holding together the crucial southern front? Was it pity because he had lost his family despite having loved them so dearly? Was it jealousy because FB was so popular among the rank and file of the forces, for his larger-than-life image and reputation?

During the Catsmash purge, several PRC rank holders had asked Kapo to send FB to the pit. They hated his utter disregard for their orders, his irreverence and his eccentric ways, his popularity among the soldiers, his disdain for the party hierarchy. But Kapo has never been able to bring himself to obey that order. He could not send the friend who'd taken a bullet in the back for him to the firing squad. So he admired him in private, was concerned about him. To the PRC Brigadiers and Generals who'd asked for his head, Kapo had said, 'I'm not going to do a Stalin on Trotsky.'

And as Yusuf had said, 'You'll have to ask one of these Generals to pull the trigger. No soldier's going to fire a shot at Comrade Firebrand.'

IV

Usually the first thing President Adam Bum did when he woke up at 9.30 was to check the stock price of Bum Realty Corp. But not today. An upset tummy had him rushing to the toilet at 4 a.m. Come to think of it, bowel trouble is a great leveller. Even the most powerful man on the planet is reduced to rushing his ass to the right place before it's too late. The President had been in and out of the toilet, pulling his flannel pyjamas up and down at regular intervals for the next two hours. He was exhausted by the time his bedside phone began to ring. He picked it up and let out a feeble 'Hello?'

'Frank here. You need to meet the rest of us asap. We're on our way to the office. This is big, Mr President. You don't want to miss this one.'

If his Secretary of State, his Defence Secretary and the Director of his intelligence agency were rushing to meet him at 7 a.m., it really must be something big. This wasn't Eurasian tanks rolling into yet another West Asian kingdom, nor that madcap Park testing another missile capable of landing on the City of Lights. 'Or has that crazy piece of shit actually launched one at us?' he wondered in the shower. A major terror leader droned? An alien invasion of Earth? A video of one of his orgies gone public? Bum walked into the meeting his head abuzz with possibilities.

'What's the matter?' he said, sitting down at the table.

'Something strange happened on Monday night, Bummer,' said Frank. 'We think you should know about it. You remember our stock of slightly-outdated-but-still-operational warfighting equipment in our reserve inventory?'

Bum nodded.

'The whole damn lot's gone missing. Across thousands of locations, every plane, rifle, tank, artillery, bomb, shell, missile, launcher—all gone. None of the facilities, high-security ones, were broken into. The sensors picked up nothing. Nor the cameras. Nor the guards. Looks like they were all disabled for the duration of the heist.'

Bum looked at Frank in disbelief.

'Something similar happened in Eurasia,' said Shane, 'I was just reading about it.'

'When?' Bum asked.

'In the last 24 hours, Mr President. All over Europe, Canada, Australia, Japan, China—you name it,' said Liz. 'Everywhere.'

'And not one satellite anywhere has picked up anything,' Shane continued, his voice troubled. 'Such a large consignment of weapons—laid down, they'd cover the whole of Spain and

France. And nothing anywhere, on any system. We've covered every square inch of the planet, but it seems millions and millions of weapons have simply vanished. This is unprecedented, Mr President.'

'No organization or government in the world can pull off such an operation across the globe in 24 hours. So what do we do, Frank? How do we keep it from the media?'

'Deny the whole thing, as always,' Frank said with a laugh, then quickly grew serious again. 'If this gets out, we'll be in deep shit. Can't blame the ragheads for breaking into the world's most secure vaults and making away with millions of weapons on World Island soil.'

'Maybe we could blame it on the aliens,' said Bum to the utter astonishment of the other three.

'Don't be an ass, Bummer,' snapped Frank, 'This can't get out. That's the long and the short of it. We'll only know who's responsible once the weapons are used somewhere.'

The three mandarins got up to leave. Liz turned to face Bum, 'By the way, Mr President, we're getting the Lunch Box into Sands as we had planned. Just keeping you posted.'

'Oh yeah. Is the food any good? Has anyone tasted it?'

'The Rockie Club scientists claim so. In a controlled experiment, it went off like clockwork. Hopefully, we don't have to test the real thing.'

'Who's on the job?'

'A young lad, Ivy League. Brilliant student of mathematics and philosophy. Immigrant child, he was 13 then. Republic-origin. Very sharp, one of our best recruits. He'll blend in well with the locals, speaks the language too.'

'Good, good. I can't wait to know the result of the feed.'

'It's an absolutely last resort, Mr President. I hope you remember that,' Liz gave him a hard look and walked quickly out of the room.

V

It was one of those days when the sun and the clouds had not entered into a clear pact over control of the sky. And taking advantage of this lack of understanding, a brown haze had staked its claim over the atmosphere. It was a relatively quiet day in the city. The air-raid siren had gone off an hour ago, and most residents had decided to stay indoors. The usual bustle of the market was absent, and only a few people lined up for bread in front of Afghan Bakery run by Old Halil down the street. Four street dogs scrabbled about in the dustbin outside Maharani Tea House.

All 79 members of the Military Council were in their chairs by 9.30 a.m., sipping their coffee. General Bahadur was reminding everyone about his great-grandfather, a Victoria Cross awardee, and how every generation of his family since the eleventh century had given birth to warriors. In-between, he was casting lecherous glances at Brigadier Maria, more specifically at her breasts. His temper wasn't helped by the fact that she was ignoring him and staring instead at Colonel Firebrand standing at the window, smoking with his back to the room.

Brigadier Nagaraju was busy showing off his prosthetic leg, now apparently almost a natural extension of his body. A pensive General Salman was busy arranging his files on procurements, orders and arrivals. He kept jumbling them up, and managed to get their order right after a full six attempts. Then he put the weight of his heavy hands on them with such nervousness that you'd think they were about to grow legs and run out of the room just to have some fun.

It was then that El Comandante walked in. Everyone stood up. Firebrand was already standing. He took two or three more puffs of his cigarette, stubbed it out, tossed it through the window and turned.

'The 52nd meeting of the Central Military Council is now in session. El Comandante will address the meeting,' declared Brigadier Monet just as General Salman, by way of fanfare no doubt, let out one of his noisy farts. There were chuckles all around. Kapo climbed onto the stage, fixing his angry gaze at those who were laughing. 'Dear comrades and fellow journeymen, let me thank you all for your perseverance and your devotion to the cause and struggle of the PRC Guerrillas. You have been fighting against all odds and have kept the Republican forces at bay with meagre resources.'

No one but Firebrand saw the six enormous birds of prey glide into the theatre. But at the sound of flapping wings, everyone looked up at the ceiling. Kapo took a few seconds to overcome his surprise and speak again: 'I can almost picture the day when our struggle will bear fruit, I can see victory close at hand. The Republican forces are demoralized—'

'Bullshit,' growled a voice from the back of the theatre. Everybody turned around but they could only see a pair of yellow eyes glowing in the dark. There was a moment of silence, and then a soldier tried to train his Kalashnikov at the source of the voice. But one of the roosting ospreys was quicker, and a powerful peck on the guard's hand was enough. Before the man could regain his balance, and the others could understand what was happening, a giant black panther leapt onto the table with a roar and landed on it with the smoothness of a ballerina. Its tail lashed out at Brigadier Gogoi, flicking the pistol out of his hand. Then it lifted its head and looked straight at the Brigadier: 'If I had used my paw, you would have one less hand to use, you fool.'

Black Panther looked up at the stage. 'Get your fat ass down here now. I don't have all day.'

The room was silent and absolutely still. El Comandante gaped at Firebrand for a few moments, then stumbled down the steps and fell into a chair.

'The fact of the matter is that you chaps have done a pretty good job of squeezing the balls of the Republican forces. But soon the odds against you are going to be insurmountable. That is where we come into the picture. That is why I have been sent to speak to you. Any questions?'

'Who is this *we* you are referring to?' asked El Comandante.

'Are the Republican forces moving their navy and reserve-strike corps?' General Bahadur blurted out.

'Yes, they are. They are moving guided missile destroyers and the flat top with 60 aircraft. And their reserve strike corps, six mechanized brigades as well as two active ones. But that is not the end of your troubles, I'm afraid. And Kapo, the answer to your question is not that simple. You will have to wait and find out.'

El Comandante looked at Firebrand and General Bahadur, both of whom looked distinctly worried. They had reason to be. While the PRC Guerrillas had the capability to hold their own against a limited ground offensive, they did not have the wherewithal to target warships floating hundreds of nautical miles away on the high seas, brimming with deadly precision-strike weapons.

'To hold off a combined offensive of four strike corps,' Firebrand looked at the nervous faces around the table as he spoke, 'We need to defend with proper formations. And that means we'll be sitting ducks for those cruise missiles launched from the ships. We need to get bodies across the seas and sink those ships. That's our only hope.'

'Now, the bigger bad news,' Black Panther chuckled and his whiskers wiggled to and fro. 'Seven days from now, World Island will come forward with military support for the Republic. It will send two of its most expansive fleets, with four supercarriers. Plus, a large number of Walrus Special Forces and intelligence operatives, three infantry and two armoured divisions. The ships have set sail three days ago, and are entering the Indian Ocean as I speak. The deployment is barely a week away.'

Utter pandemonium broke out. World Island was the strongest military and economic power. It had hundreds and hundreds of warships, over ten thousand combat aircraft, a three-million-strong army and a plethora of sophisticated arms and weapons which most countries could only dream of possessing. Four out of every five Global 500 companies were headquartered there.

'If World Island enters the picture, we will have no option but to surrender,' said the usually reticent General Salman.

'No retreat, no surrender,' thundered Firebrand and slammed his fist down on the table. 'Surrender is not an option. We will only end up in the firing line. I would rather go down in action than eat lead with my hands tied behind my back!'

'Calm down, everyone,' said Brigadier Maria, 'if the World Island does come to the aid of the Republic, perhaps we can enlist the support of Eurasia. Don't lose hope. We've come this far. It's not for nothing.'

Black Panther grinned, and the light hit his fangs with a glint, 'I'm relieved that someone's thinking straight. But the Eurasians are not going to intervene. They may send you some arms, but that's all. They have their hands full in West Asia and on their own border.'

Firebrand nodded, 'Such a large deployment essentially translates into a naval blockade. The only way we can receive Eurasian arms are via the mountain passes in the Arakanis Heights. And our enemies will keep a hawk's eye on the place, maybe even deploy dedicated satellites to watch over the route. It won't be easy.'

Black Panther pounded his right paw like a gavel on the table. 'Listen, soldiers. Weapons, ammunition and money won't be hindrances. You don't have to worry about them. Just make sure you stand together and give them a hell of a fight. I have to go now. Firebrand, maybe you can tell this lot about the orders you've received from us. Follow them and you'll make history, people.'

Black Panther turned and leapt over Firebrand's head and out through the window, followed by the flock of ospreys who had been perched silently near the ceiling all this while. Brigadier Banerjea rushed to the window only to see them vanish into the brown haze.

'Colonel Firebrand,' Kapo spoke after a few minutes of stunned silence, 'you are now General Firebrand. The PRC Guerrilla 1st Strike Corps and 4th Reserve Corps are now under your command. General Bahadur will be in charge of the 3rd Strike Corps as usual. Firebrand is our best bet to beat these odds. Any questions?'

There seemed to be none, though judging by some faces, not everyone was happy with the decision.

'General Firebrand is our most experienced battle commander,' General Bahadur spoke up, 'He has handled brigade and division-level operations before with considerable elan. His name strikes fear in the heart of the enemy. This is the right move.'

'Unbelievable. A beast of the jungle has just told us how to plan our battle,' El Comandante put his head down on the table.

'At least someone has,' said Maria, getting up, walking over to the window and lighting one of her long black cigarettes.

'Can I nick a smoke?' asked Firebrand.

'How can a Brigadier refuse a General? But careful, these are clove-flavoured.'

'Sounds about right for someone with a sore throat.'

Firebrand took a cigarette off the pack, and soon he and Maria were blowing smoke out of the window and up into the sky. Firebrand's mind was already at the frontline. If there were more than four strike corps coming at them, they certainly could not afford to let the attackers reach them. They would simply get rolled over.

'So, how do we stop such an overwhelming force, FB?' asked Maria.

'When they come, we will welcome them with a layered defence comprising minefields, zigzag trenches, anti-tank ditches, dragon's teeth and concrete pill boxes. Defend till you can. And then fall back to the next layer. That will negate their numerical advantage in armour and manpower. But we need to get this done in about 10 days. That's the tough part.' Then he stroked his beard, said goodbye to Maria and left.

As he came out, Kapo was waiting. 'FB, tell me you have a plan.'

'I do. But I will need many diggers, compactors and excavators and lots of men with digging tools, lots and lots of them.'

'You got it, Comrade. All in for victory.'

Firebrand got into the backseat of his jeep, took off his hat and nodded at Kapo as the wheels began to roll.

VI

When Purple Backpack landed in a military airport, 100 kilometres from the western frontiers of Sands, it was close to midnight. A bald man with a distinguished moustache and an even more distinguished paunch met him on the tarmac and led him to a car. Handing over a large yellow envelope, a small suitcase and a heavy camera bag, he held out his hand, 'Hi, I'm Ted. Ted Lytton, South Asia Desk, Tantilash. You are . . . ' The flight from Tantilash was not long but Purple Backpack was tired—he had been on a 16-hour nonstop commercial flight already and then a wait in-between, and then this flight. And he had to be ready quite early the next morning. 'My friends call me Purple Backpack,' he said. 'Please keep the consignment safe and good to travel. I have to be off at seven, sharp.'

'It will be. The car will take you to where you're staying the night. You've got all you need in there.'

'Thanks,' said Purple Backpack. 'I'd sent a request for a four-wheel drive, muddy and dirty, with the papers in my passport name, though spelt just a little differently.'

'I'll bring the beauty over at six with all the paperwork. Also, the lens case and the lens in the middle have been made to the specifications you had asked for. Now get in the car. Get some food, get some sleep. See you in the morning.'

Once he arrived at the guest house, Purple Backpack strode into his room, emptied the suitcase onto the bed, then scramble-tucked all his things into the rucksack in a deliberately sloppy manner. Then he opened the camera bag and brought out the Canon body. Switched it on, checked some of the pictures on the card. Satisfied, he put it back and brought out the heavy lens case. Three threateningly expensive lenses stared up at him. He brought out two of them, the first and the third. Then gently pressed down a part of the middle one and slid it inside the cushioning fabric. The entire panel came off, and Purple Backpack beamed at what lay inside. A Beretta 92FS. He brought it out and sniffed at the mouth of the barrel. Then reversed the magazine-release button with his Swiss knife, 'Everyone assumes the world is right-handed . . . ' He put in one of the magazines and dangled the pistol from the index finger of his left hand. It felt good. He had a thing for the 92 from his training days. To him, it was the most reliable son of a gun. The open-slide design allowed easy clearing of obstructions, and it always shot true.

Next, he brought out the miniature satellite phone and tested it. It worked perfectly on scramble signature.

Repacking the camera bag, he finally went for a shower. By the time he emerged, a hot meal of rice, lentil soup and mutton curry was waiting for him.

'Sir, what would you like to drink?' asked the caretaker.

'Do you have any juice?'

'Only apple and orange, sir. But I can get you some fresh coconut water.'

'Great. Also, I have an early start. I'd like breakfast at 6.30, please.'

'No problem, sir.'

Waiting for the coconut water to arrive, Purple Backpack made a call.

'Hello, Mamma. Efflestone service is lousy in Cambodia, and I have to take a local number. I'll call you when I can.'

He listened patiently while his mother spoke.

'Don't worry, Mamma. I won't keep a lot of cash with me. Please stop reading all that stuff on the internet and getting nervous. I'm a big boy now, OK? I can take care of myself. In any case, I'm not alone, the entire programme team is here.'

He paused again.

'OK, Mamma, love you. Don't worry too much. I'll email you. Over and out.'

Purple Backpack dived into his dinner and devoured it in 10 minutes flat. Back in his room, he took out a sim card from the yellow envelope and slid it into his cell phone. He took out the cash and the cards and organized them neatly in his wallet. The cards and cash from his wallet and the SIM card he'd used to call his mother went into the yellow envelope. He put his phone on charge. Set an alarm for 6 a.m. Then shut his eyes and fell asleep at once.

VII

When the combined task force of the Republican Navy and the World Island Navy started closing in on Sands from the south, Admiral Ramon Limpdick, commander of the joint fleet comprising 60 warships (including six aircraft carriers), sat down with the satellite grabs and video footage of the PRC Guerrillas' defence installations on the southern coast. While he could see armed formations on the west with armour, air defence, artillery and infantry engaged in pitched battle with the joint land forces, there were no visible defences he could find towards the south.

'Am I seeing things right, Varun? There are no defences in the south. We could have the Marines and Walrus forces land on the beaches with air cover and wipe the field in a matter of hours. They won't be able to deploy troops from the west that fast. Even if they do, their defences will thin out and we'll be on their tail from two ends. In a week or two, we'll be in Calcutta. Once their capital falls, the resistance will crumble in a few days, weeks at most.'

'Game, set and match, Admiral,' said Vice-Admiral Varun Choksi, commander of the Eastern Fleet.

'But what are they doing, Varun? So many men and women digging the earth, putting iron poles into the ground? What the hell are they up to?'

'The PRC animals must be slave-driving them. Keeping them busy with stupid earthwork. Whoever refuses will be shot. Animals, I tell you.'

'But I can see PRC soldiers digging too. See, here, one of the women is kissing a soldier, and they're having a laugh. Some even seem to be singing. Doesn't look like slave-driving to me, Varun. These buggers are up to something we're not being able to gauge.'

'They're ignorant village folk, brutes, I tell you. They think they can stop this might with iron poles and small arms. We'll crush them like roaches.'

'You're missing my point. Have you seen what they're digging along? There are markings, can you see? Uniform lines running for hundreds and hundreds of miles. Like the Nazca lines, multiplied hundredfold. They weren't there even a week back.'

'What lines?'

'Nazca lines. Peru.'

'I don't know much about Africa, to be honest.'

'Peru's not in Africa, Varun. It's in South America.'

'Whatever. Anyway, why are you so bothered with these markings?'

'Because 900 miles of these lines have appeared in a week, and these guys are digging along them. It's strange, very strange. And by the way, with your kind of geographical knowledge, how did you become Vice-Admiral?'

'Because I have the right contacts, and the Republican Navy never ventures out of the Indian Ocean,' Varun grinned impishly. 'I've got to go back to my ship now. Have to call my wife in an hour. Got to keep the Home Ministry happy all the time.'

'See you when I see you, Varun.'

'Yes, Admiral. By the way, when will you introduce me to your second officer?'

'Go back to your ship. You have a woman waiting at home for your call. It's not good for a family man to have a roving eye.'

'OK, Admiral.'

As Choksi left, Limpdick went back to studying the images with his intel officer, Phil. 'Prepare a report on these lines. I want a proper timeline, covering the last week. I'd like it by this evening, please.'

Limpdick ordered his lunch in the command room itself. It was an early one. He'd had a disturbed night and wanted an afternoon nap. He picked at the Thai beef salad while poring over the maps and images. Then he proceeded towards his living quarters.

As he opened the door to his suite and closed it behind him, a strange smell hit him. If Limpdick had ever worked in a zoo, he would have identified it right away. Then he spotted his prized possession, a bottle of Martell's Premier Voyage, a gift from the French Defence Minister, lying uncorked and quarter empty on his study table. The drinks-cabinet door was ajar.

He turned left and opened the sliding door to his bedroom, but saw no one. Though the porthole was open, which was unusual. His bedsheets were crumpled and the pillows tossed about. The strange smell grew stronger. He headed to the porthole to pull it shut but froze as a voice growled, 'Sit down, Limpdick.'

Limpdick took a moment or two to unfreeze his limbs and turn around. Seated in his armchair was Black Panther, who took a sip of the 15,000-dollar cognac and put the snifter down on the left armrest. 'Now, that's what I call a good brandy. It's too bad they produced just 300 decanters of it. Don't you think so?'

Limpdick slowly turned his head to glance at the hook on the left wall where his Sig Sauer P320 usually hung from its holster. He saw the holster but not the gun. Then he saw another snifter, filled to the right height, placed on top of the chest of drawers against that same wall.

'Looking for this, Limpdick?' Black Panther put down the pistol beside the snifter. 'Never bring a gun to a party, Admiral. Now, pick up that glass. Let's have a drink together.'

The Admiral had no choice but to do as he was told. He badly needed a drink anyway.

'That's a good lad, Limpdick. I'm going to tell you what those guys in Sands are up to. I'm going to tell you a lot more than your birdbrain will be able to process from Phil's report. I'm also going to tell you what will happen to you, your men and women, and your majestic ships. But, first, chin-chin.'

Black Panther lifted the snifter with his right paw and held it out at the Admiral. 'Cheers. To the good times.'

Black Panther took a big sip, then licked his whiskers. 'Now, you must have realized that 997 miles of geoglyphs can't appear overnight. It's humanly impossible, a mathematical reality that's highly improbable, though statistically possible. If you check your satellite feed between 12.34 a.m. and 12.35 a.m. last Saturday, it's ka-fucking-boom. They're not there. And in a minute, they are. You getting me, sailor?'

'Yes,' Limpdick tried his best to sound in control. In his youth, he'd been a champion boxer at the Naval Academy and was still as strong as an ox. And to be honest, he wasn't as much afraid as he was in shock, experiencing utter disbelief rather than cold terror. Black Panther was too suave and civil to frighten him, though the size of his paws and fangs were not to be entirely ignored.

'Listen, Limpdick, as a military commander, I am sure the lives and well-being of your men and women matter to you, yes?'

Limpdick nodded.

'So it is my, rather our, humble advice to you to let them know that they're not going home. Neither are you. Yes, it's hard to believe, I know, with all this technology and all these weapons at your disposal. But you're having this conversation with Black Panther over some damn fine brandy in the middle of the ocean. That itself should tell you that you're not in command, Admiral.'

'So, you think that ragtag force will defeat my soldiers?' Limpdick said, unable to stop himself, 'You think those PRC rebels are any match for my force?'

'Limpdick, do you really think that you're up against only the PRC outlaws here? And when did I talk about fighting or bloodshed? I simply said: you're here, and you're not going home. You're up against something that's well beyond the scope of your understanding. You see, when time resets the clock, you're just wisps of straw waiting to be blown away, to be remade as parts of a new puzzle. So, be a good boy and tell that Bummer: He will lose every ship and everything and everyone on board. And there is nothing he can do to stop it.'

Limpdick gaped as Black Panther downed the cognac, climbed down from the armchair and gave him a pat on his shoulder. 'It was good to see you, sailor. See you in the new world.'

Black Panther climbed onto Limpdick's bed and leapt out through the open porthole. Four giant long-horned birds swooped down on him, and then they all disappeared into the clouds, flanked by a convocation of eagles. To the Admiral, it looked like a C-17 Globemaster being escorted by a group of F-15s.

VIII

The earthwork all along Sand's borders was in full swing. So was the battle for Devil's Lair, being waged on the banks of the Ganges. The PRC Guerrillas, under General Firebrand's command, had been subject to intense aerial bombardment; the losses had been heavy. While the PRC surface-to-air missile batteries had been successfully dealing with the Republican Air Force and World Island Air Force's Generation 4-Plus planes, they had little answer for the radar-evading stealth planes. Yes, they shot down four, but there were far too many.

The houses, especially those on the riverfront, looked like ghostly creatures with a thousand empty eyes, the holes left by anti-material gunfire and mortar shells. The structures that had been subject to regular shelling had larger holes, like mouths waiting to swallow you up. The men and women who survived the onslaught came back later to salvage what they could from the wreckage. Some of them lit a torch in the evenings or late nights to look for their valuables, only to be picked off by snipers lying in wait on the other side of the river. Such was the bandobast.

Even so, the Republican Army, backed by World Island's ground forces, could not break down the PRC Guerrilla resistance. Both the land and railway bridges across the river had been blown away by the Guerrillas before they retreated to this side of the river. The Republican Armed Forces had sent in waves of armoured and motorized infantry assaults across another bridge that lay 200 kilometres to the north. But, by then, the infamous monsoons of the east had already set in. Since the roads were peppered with mines and improvised explosive devices, cutting across the countryside remained the only option. But the heavy tanks and infantry fighting vehicles kept getting stuck in the mud and slush, and became sitting ducks for RPGs and anti-tank missiles. The Republican sol-diers, hailing mainly from the northern heartland, were not used to such heavy rains. On top of that, their rifles and carbines, all M-series, began to malfunction with alarming regularity. Walking for weeks through the jungle and across fields, their feet sinking into the sticky mud with every step, had exhausted them. Fevers and stomach troubles plagued them every step of the way.

The rains brought with them snakes and scorpions and large bugs with vicious bites. And the Guerrillas made good use of their natural allies. Recalling Ho Chi Minh's famous words, General Firebrand announced on Radio Liberation: 'Not only every man and woman, the old and the children, will resist the evil forces' attempt to run Sands over. Every animal, reptile and insect inhabiting this land will also play its part in this heroic struggle of resistance.'

At night, the Guerrillas would silently swim across the river with large clay pots whose mouths were sealed with cloth. These pots were hurled inside the trenches and the dugouts of the enemy. Upon impact, the pots would break and venomous snakes would wriggle out, hissing with fury. More enemy soldiers died from their own panic fire than they did of snakebite.

It was at such a time that Madame President decided to replace Lieutenant General D. G. Bakshi, Commander, Operation Domination, with General Dalpreet Singh, a career infantryman who had the respect of the best of the Republican Army's fighting units. He hailed from a warrior community, a pedigree Bakshi did not have. Madame President thought Singh could be a catalyst in turning the fortunes of the war in her favour.

Singh arrived, studied the situation and sent his report to Dodi. In his opinion, a direct assault across the river on Devil's Lair by laying bridges was nothing but suicide. The bridge 200 kilometres to the north was their best bet. Earlier operations had failed because the bridgehead they had been trying to establish in order to launch the 90-degree-turn attack had been too narrow. 'A 200- to 300-metre-wide bridgehead is barely enough to sustain an incursion. I am not even going to imagine the horrid conditions of our troops when faced with a counterattack. The narrow bridgehead allowed the PRC forces to shell our flanks much in the manner of target practice. I intend to establish a wider bridgehead, at least 3 kilometres wide, before launching our attack.'

'Your game, Dalpreet,' came the swift response from Tantilash, 'Do what you feel is right. I want Calcutta to fall before winter comes.'

The General rallied support from the Army commandos and Para Special Forces units as well as the World Island Walrus companies. Since armoured or motorized movement was restricted, he decided on a shock-and-awe infantry attack by highly skilled marksmen and area-domination companies. The idea: to kill by combining surprise and superior firepower.

So, one fateful morning, when the rain had stopped for a while, more than 2,000 commandos, Para and Walrus forces, assisted by another 4,000 of the most battle-hardened infantrymen, launched the assault on the PRC Guerrillas guarding the mouth of the bridge. Operation First Flush was on.

As soon as they realized the depth of their enemy's firepower, the Guerrillas retreated into the forest that began just 500 metres away. Undeterred, Dalpreet's men pursued them with full gusto. The Guerrillas ran deeper into the trees. Dalpreet was delighted; this perfectly coincided with his tactic of trying to widen the bridgehead. Once the 6,000 invading soldiers were firmly inside the jungle, another 600 arrived to consolidate the open ground near the bridge. The General, now assured of holding on to the bridgehead, ordered a full-scale pursuit of the Guerrillas still scattering deeper and deeper into the forest.

And that proved to be the undoing of the Republican Army.

Following instructions from Major Aks, the PRC Guerrillas climbed the trees and assumed positions. Then, at the right moment, they slashed at the ropes tied to the high branches—

and hundreds of beehives, wrapped in mosquito nets, dropped all across the forest onto the Republican Army soldiers. Some of them tried to run back towards the open ground, but were felled by the swarms of stinging bees. Many dived into the bushes and the maize fields on either side of the forest paths. But those had been prepared too—with thousands of sharpened bamboo spikes. The Guerrillas took more than 1,500 prisoners of war that day and looted all the weapons and ammo.

Only 700 soldiers made it back across the bridge to join the 600 waiting there to hold the bridgehead.

The next day, a White Flag meet was held in the middle of the bridge. The Guerrillas handed over 3,800 bodies to the Republican Army. The mass impaling of some of the toughest men of the Republican Army and World Island Special Forces sent shockwaves rippling through the world. Even the World Island Army commanders were shocked. General Dalpreet Singh ran up a high fever, and Madame President skipped dinner despite her favourite fish being on the menu. This was not the way the script was supposed to play out, especially not after Nida Dodi had roped in the World Islanders on her side.

She called Bum that night. 'Mr President, you have the Lunch Box in position?'

'Yes, my dear. Why do you ask?'

'I think the time has come.'

'I know, but I still have to consult some folks back here. I am standing for re-election, you understand that, right?'

'Yes. But if things continue like this, we may not have an Army left before too long. A fitting answer needs to be given.'

'I agree. I'll call my commanders right away. By the way, I read a report claiming most of their sniper kills were from a Second World War bullet. Do you know anything about that?'

'No, but I'll find out.'

'Patience, my dear. We will win the war, and we will have our Special Economic Zone. Don't worry.'

'Good night.'

'Good night, my dear.'

When the Republican Army and World Island doctors had examined the bodies, they had been taken aback by the 7.62x54mmR sniper bullets lodged in most of the victims. 'These used to be fired from Mosin–Nagant guns by Soviet snipers in the Second World War. How did these rebels get them?' wondered Brigadier Dr Ed Shapiro.

The PRC Guerrillas were amazed at the number of sniper kills too, because they had deployed only a dozen. The snipers themselves were dumbfounded—when they tried to tally their hits, they arrived at around 180 kills at the most.

So how did the extra bodies fall? wondered Aks.

Nevertheless, it was a moment of glory. At the field base, a party was thrown to honour the snipers' superlative feat. After an hour or so, a dozen Caucasian men and women carrying ancient guns fitted with iron sights walked in, went up to the bar and asked for a vodka each.

Aks was curious about the strangers. He went up to them. 'I don't think we've met?'

'Vasily Zaitsev,' said one.

'Lyudmila Pavlichenko,' said a young woman to the right.

'Roza Shanina,' said another woman, standing beside Lyudmila.

Aks, already three drinks down, burst out laughing.

'You don't have to believe us,' said Lyudmila, 'but you do know that all those sniper kills were not by your men, right? Call Firebrand, he'll clear your head.'

Aks hurried aside and called up Firebrand. Firebrand heard him out, and then said, 'Honour them. Each one of them has hundreds of kills in the Second World War, Aks. Make sure we have enough vodka.'

That night, it was one long and fierce party.

In the wee hours of the morning, as they prepared to leave, Vasily called the PRC snipers together: 'If you have a strong breeze blowing to the right and your target is more than 500 metres away, shoot an inch to the left of your target. That way, you'll never waste a bullet.'

Roza gave Aks a kiss on his lips.

'I'd never ever imagined I'd kiss a ghost,' said Aks.

'We're not that bad, young man. And you know the best part about making out with a ghost?'

'No, I hell don't.'

'You don't have to worry about bad breath.'

IX

Limpdick got off the phone with President Bum, seething with anger. And got onto the fleet's public-announcement system right away:

'Men and women, the PRC Guerrillas have martyred hundreds and hundreds of our Special Forces. Many of them have been impaled in the most barbaric manner. The President wants us to show them what World Island stands for. What it means to have attacked its armed forces. What consequences that brings. What price they have to pay. Prepare, soldiers. As dusk falls today, we will light up Sands. There will be no night for Sands tonight. It will be all light. We will rain hell on them. We will show them that there is only one thing worse than God's wrath. And that is the World Island's fury.'

The pilots went to work. The maintenance crew, the bomb loaders swung into action.

Varun Choksi called up Nida Dodi. 'Madame President, you do not have to worry any more. I think they are going to flatten Calcutta and Sands tonight.'

'I'll believe it when I see it, Choksi.'

Many hundreds of kilometres away, in the courtyard of a derelict house in a dirty lane in the rebels' self-declared capital of Calcutta, Marshal Bhodi was lying on a charpoy, his bare belly staring up at the overcast sky. A red-and-white-chequered gamchha covered his face. After a more-than-sumptuous meal of rice and spicy small-crab curry, he was now deeply and blissfully asleep.

A little distance away, Naren, his squire, was busy rinsing cheap anti-lice shampoo off his hair.

Bhodi's wife Bechamoni was seated on the stairs that led up to their two or three rooms on the ground floor, playing Ludo by herself. One of the rooms did not have a window, and its door was always tightly locked.

'Bechu,' Bhodi suddenly stirred, and called out to her lovingly from his charpoy.

'What do you want?' Bechamoni asked without looking up, busy rolling the dice in a small plastic tumbler.

'Will you come and stroke my tummy a bit? It's making strange noises.'

'I have told you again and again not to be such a hog with the crab curry. You never listen,' she said, but moved a little closer to him and gently caressed his belly with one hand.

After a while, she said, 'Ai, listen no. We haven't been to the movies in so long. Will you take me to one?'

'Which one?'

'Let's go to the movie hall and decide. Just like old times.'

'Yes, Bechu, let's go,' Bhodi said, pulling Bechamoni close, running his fingers through her hair.

'Don't drink tonight. You have a talking tummy. It's almost 5.30. Shall I get you some tea?'

'Yes, why not?'

Bechamoni got up and went into the house to make tea. Bhodi sat up, contentedly scratching his crotch. Then went over to the tap in the wall and splashed some water on his face. He wiped it dry with the gamchha and was stretching his bones when Bechamoni arrived with three cups of tea and a plate full of Marie biscuits.

'Naren, here's your tea,' she called out.

Naren took his cup and sat in a corner as Bhodi and Bechamoni sat down with theirs on the charpoy. And that's when Raven landed in their courtyard.

Bhodi and Bechamoni folded their hands and bowed their heads.

'Father,' said Bhodi reverentially, 'how have you been?'

'How does it matter to you, scumbag? Naren, two glasses, my drinking bowl, the bottle and some water—right now. How are you, my beautiful daughter-in-law, married to my worthless son?'

A few of you readers may know Raven as Dondobayosh.

'I am fine, Father, just a bit under the weather,' said Bechamoni, pulling the edge of her saree over her head.

'Tell me about it—I've got such a runny nose.'

A mean-looking Civet Cat ambled down the roof, along with an elderly lady, dressed like an eighteenth-century noble-woman, smoking a cigarette stuck into a silver holder.

Naren brought out some plastic stools, and they all sat down.

Now, some of you readers may also know that Civet Cat is none other than Bonberal, and the elderly lady is Begum Johnson. It really does not matter if you do not. Now, you do. If you google Begum Johnson, you will see that her grandson Robert Jenkinson went on to become the Prime Minister of England and steered the country through the turbulence of the post–Napoleonic Wars era.

Now: back to the courtyard.

Raven gulped down the fermented-rice alcohol and turned to Bhodi. 'What are we, Bhodi?'

'We are the descendants of Atmaram Sarkar, Father.'

'Next, you'll tell me you look somewhat like a cross between an ape and a human, and that your father is a raven, you dimwit. We are known by what we do. Don't state the obvious.'

'We are saucerers, we are the saucer masters, masters of saucery,' exclaimed Bechamoni.

'Shut up, cow,' hissed Bhodi, 'Can't you see the men are talking here? Go inside.'

Raven rushed at Bhodi and gave him a resounding slap with his wings. 'If you dare talk like that to my daughter-in-law again, I'll skin you alive. She gave the right answer.'

Bhodi boxed his own ears. 'Forgive me, Father.'

'It is her you should ask forgiveness from.'

'Bechu, I am sorry. You are not angry with me, no?'

'I feel bad when you tell me off like that just because I am a woman. But I am not angry. Naren, please get our guests some muri, to have with their drinks.'

'Sexist pig, I tell you. Can't believe he came off my semen. Now,' Raven continued, 'As you know, Bhodi, we saucerers do not break with family traditions. But these are exceptional times.'

'I am sure, Father. You would never take a decision without due consideration.'

'So, in a minute from now, when the moth hour sets in, you will open the Chamber of Saucers. It is the call of the time, and our friends need our help. This is our last hurrah, Bhodi. Set the saucers free.'

'Father, I wish to remind you that we last opened it towards the beginning of the 2000s. So, we should wait till the early 2100s at least. And do you mean to say that we won't call the saucers back? That we'll set them free?'

'I know all that, Bhodi. But history will not absolve us if we do not play our part now. This is it. The greatest show on earth is unfolding in front of us. This is the time. This is our final deed. Set them free. Unlock the Chamber of Saucers!'

Bechamoni began to dance around the courtyard in a frenzy. Bhodi put a slash of vermillion on her forehead, on

Naren's forehead too. Begum Johnson began to dance with Bechamoni, though her steps were more of a measured waltz. Naren held out a bunch of keys towards Bhodi. Bhodi grabbed them and proceeded towards the room without a window. The heavy lock finally came off, the door creaked open. And hundreds and hundreds of dazzling-bright, razor-thin saucers, some as small as a fidget spinner, some as large as a car tyre, began to spin out of the room. They spun around the courtyard while Bhodi and Naren clapped, and Bechamoni, Begum Johnson and Raven danced below them.

Then the saucers lifted off, and in a trice, vanished into the sky.

X

Purple Backpack was 40 kilometres away from Calcutta and feeling sleepy behind the wheel. He had been criss-crossing the length and breadth of Sands in his Isuzu pick-up, shooting pictures of birds even though he was least interested in them. But he did enjoy driving to new places, meeting new people, the amazing conversations he'd have all along the way. Somewhere deep inside, he had begun to form a new perspective on the civil war, something that had not been possible when he'd only read the news reports in the Western media and the intelligence inputs presented to him before his mission.

He'd crossed Border Control with little difficulty, and the PRC units he'd encountered in most places had been cordial. A few of the soldiers had even suggested areas he should visit if he wanted pictures of the usually evasive spotted eagle. Some had shared their meals with him. What had surprised him was that, at the small roadside food and tea shacks, the soldiers always paid for their meals and drinks. It did not seem to him that people in Sands were living under the fear of the gun. He reported as much to his HQ, not that it made any difference to the big picture.

He met cobblers, artisans, mendicant musicians, truck drivers, hooch peddlers, landless labourers, out-of-work dock-yard loaders, teachers, holy men . . . And every time he was amazed that while they were fully aware that the prospects of a PRC victory was remote, they still preferred to go down fighting and not submit meekly to Madame President's whims and fancies.

Since he was feeling sleepy, he stopped at a tea shack, splashed some water on his face and ordered tea in broken Hindi. A few young men were seated round a table, and he asked them if he could sit beside them. Once the tea arrived, they got talking.

'What is astounding is the resolve I have seen in the people here to fight against all odds, knowing they are staring at sure defeat. I have been in your country only for two weeks, you know. I wonder where you guys draw your strength from.'

'Where are you from, explorer?' the old man asked from behind the counter.

'I'm from Bruges. It's a town in the Flanders region of Belgium. I am a wildlife photographer. Documenting birds in South Asia right now.'

'Is Bruges the capital of Belgium?' asked one of the men.

'No, it's Brussels.'

'So, tell me, what would you do if, overnight, your govern-ment declared that your part of the country was going to be a Special Economic Zone? If it asked you to surrender your house, your land that your ancestors have tilled for centuries, the graveyards carrying the bones of your forefathers, the schools, the places of prayer? No warning, no discussion, no dialogue, no remorse. And when you refuse, they send in the armed forces. What would you do?'

'I would fight.'

'That's exactly what we're doing here, young man. We're fighting to stay alive, fighting to save our identity.'

'It's OK, Grandpa. No need to get preachy with a visitor,' said the youngest of the group, almost a boy. He turned to Purple Backpack. 'Mullany is one of my favourite players. Too bad Barcelona couldn't get him on board.'

'Yeah, he's pretty good,' Purple Backpack said, getting up to leave.

'Please sit down,' said one of the men. There was a firmness in his voice and a scar down the side of one eye that Purple Backpack did not miss. He also realized that about three other men had silently taken up positions behind him.

Scarface spoke again. 'Anil spoke about Mullany. Do you find him to be a good player?'

'Sorry, I don't follow soccer that much. I'm not into sports, you know.'

The man stood up, pulled out a gun and put it on the table. Then he gave Purple Backpack a cold stare. 'In Belgium, my photographer friend, they play football—not soccer. Please hand over your camera.'

Purple Backpack felt two pieces of metal press against his back. He handed over the camera to the man sitting next to him.

The man took the camera and went through the pictures. 'You shot all these?'

'Yes.'

'Your passport, please.'

Purple Backpack unbuttoned his shirt and pulled his passport out of a safety pouch strapped round his chest. The man next to him snatched it away and handed it over to Scarface. Scarface studied it and dialled a number on his cell phone.

'Hello, Captain Mathew from Army Intel, Docket Number 52234. Could you connect me to Thimaya in Newsclip Filing?'

Operator: 'The oar tells me more about movement than the ocean.'

'Though it is the sea waves that brought it ashore in the first place.'

Operator: 'Connecting, please stay on the line.'

Pause.

'Hello, Thimaya. Mathew this side. Can you tell me when the great long-horned bird died? It's urgent.'

Pause.

'Thanks,' Scarface disconnected, and turned to Anil. 'You drive this man's vehicle and follow us to HQ. Someone, get the van here and pack in this piece of shit. Do not take your guns off him till you've secured the lock.'

'What's happening? Where are you taking me?' Purple Backpack tried to sound surprised.

'We're taking you to the jungle where everyone sings like a canary,' said a grinning Anil.

'What did I do? I'm just a wildlife photographer. Call my office in Belgium. I have a website too. Please, please have a look.'

Scarface thrust his face close to Purple Backpack. 'You clicked a picture of a bird in Sands that died 10 days before you arrived in the country. You fucked up big time, mate.'

Purple Backpack's shoulders throbbed with pain as his hands were yanked behind his back and tied tightly together. A rough sack-like bag was dropped over his head. A black van screeched to a halt and he was hauled up and hurled into the back. The door shut with a bang. Purple Backpack struggled up and opened his eyes. He couldn't see a thing.

They drove for quite some time, it felt as though for many hours. Then the van stopped, he was taken out of the vehicle and made to walk 250 steps. He tried to memorize the turns just as he had been trained to. Then 50 steps down. Was he in an underground room? He still couldn't see a thing.

He sat down on the floor, his back against a cold wall. He was hungry and thirsty. He was tired. He was scared. He began to think of his mother, his friends, his home, his father whom he'd last seen 14 years ago. Then, suddenly, a door was opened. It must be a woman walking towards him, she was wearing boots, the sound of her heels was very loud. She pulled the sack off his head. It took a minute or so for Purple Backpack's eyes to adjust to the light.

In front of him stood an attractive woman in her 40s. She observed him intently for a few moments, then bent forward and lifted him up gently by his shoulders. A strong woman, Purple Backpack could tell right away from her grip.

'Let me help you sit down,' she said and guided him to a chair placed beside a table. Purple Backpack slumped into it with relief. It was his first meeting with some semblance of comfort in more than 12 hours.

'You must be hungry?'

Purple Backpack nodded.

The woman clapped her hands and a guard walked in. 'Get this young man a decent meal and some water. Untie him, he needs to eat.'

'Yes, Brigadier.'

'Hello, I'm Brigadier Maria, PRC Army Intelligence. You are?'

'My friends call me Purple Backpack.'

'An odd name. I'm sure it impresses the girls. But I'm looking for something a bit more proper, like the name your parents gave you. Do you think you can help me with that?'

Purple Backpack gave her an empty look.

'It's OK, young man. Have your dinner and then we'll talk. Do you smoke? Would you like a cigarette or a drink to wash your meal down with?'

Purple Backpack shook his head.

'OK, then, I'll be back in a bit.'

Brigadier Maria slowly walked out of the room. She was trying to put him at ease. But Purple Backpack knew she could be very, very tough if she wanted to.

Soon, two burly men marched in, alongside another carrying a tray of food. There was a finger bowl on it as well.

The two men untied him, the third said: 'Sir, please wash your hands before you eat. Thank you. Also, there is a toilet there.' He pointed to the left, and then all three of them went away.

Purple Backpack gobbled up the meal in only a few minutes. It was not great but it had been freshly made. He used the toilet. He was pacing around the room, gauging its structure and height, when the door opened again. Brigadier Maria walked in. The two burly men stayed outside, and closed the door behind her.

'There are no windows in this room if you are looking for them. Come, sit down. It is my ardent request to you not to make this unpleasant. We checked with our sources in the Belgian Embassy. Your passport is forged. Also, we found a semi-automatic pistol and a satellite phone in your bag, and a very interesting lunch box, the contents of which are being examined by our technical people as we speak. We broke the code of your satellite phone, but you'd deleted the entries. Thorough job, I have to say.'

Purple Backpack stared at her, an absolutely blank and unfazed look.

'I am looking for answers to these questions. One, who are you working for? Two, what's your mission? Three, how many of you are here? Four, where are the others? Five, what information have you sent back to your handlers?'

Purple Backpack said nothing.

'You see, young man, we are fighting an unequal war here and do not have a lot of patience.'

Purple Backpack stayed silent, and looked blankly into Brigadier Maria's eyes.

'All right, suit yourself. Don't tell me later that I didn't ask you nicely.' Brigadier Maria got up and walked out. Four men, including the two who had come earlier, walked in and closed the door. Someone bolted it shut.

After a few hours, Purple Backpack lay still on the cold, damp floor. When he regained his senses, he opened his eyes. The four men had left. He felt his body was on fire, but only darkness, no light, was visible. Then he lost consciousness again.

XI

Forty naval pilots led by Lieutenant Commanders Daniel Zonshine and Tinpot Corey took off in their F-35 Lightning stealth-fighter bombers from WIS *Enterprise* and WIS *Matt Gusby*, two of the supercarriers designated with the task of bombing Sands into submission. The mood in Admiral Limpdick's fleet was gung-ho. The aircrew and loaders had been cranking up the fine flying pieces for the last many hours, and they waved their caps and saluted as one by one the planes took off. Slogans like 'No one fucks with World Island', 'With love from World Island', 'Love time is boom time' had been hastily spray-painted onto the bombs and missile shells.

As the pilots retracted their landing gear and gained altitude, Zonshine could not help but admire the beauty of the blood-red twilight horizon, and the last rays of the sun sparkling on the emerald-green waters. He loved flying. He loved to see the world from the sky.

A famous man, he had been on the cover of *Period* magazine: 'The Bach Bomber'. The bootstrap description in fine print had been: 'One of the few good men who make sure that you sleep in peace.'

In the interview, Zonshine had spoken of his love for classical music. 'It was 4 a.m. and Gaza was asleep. It was dark, save for a few flickers here and there. Then six of us went in . . . perfect formation . . . and let our load go. The ground below, the sky above—everything lit up. All the darkness disappeared. It was so beautiful. Like a symphony. It was perfect.'

'Any composition that occurred to you at that beautiful moment?'

'Yes, the Brandenburg Concertos. Bach is my go-to man, you see.'

The men flew for 10 minutes. It was nearly dark. In another five, they would disengage from their formation and move towards the predesignated coordinates to strike. It was then that Zonshine heard Corey on the radio: 'Daniel, do you see those flickering lights straight ahead? Is your radar picking up anything?'

Zonshine was surprised. There was not a blip on his radar, but he could now see the lights too. 'They seem to be flying at a similar altitude, Corey, and they're closing in—fast.'

'Break out, boys—prepare for combat,' cried out Corey but he was too late. The 40 top-gun aviators saw hundreds of flying saucers zip past them, over them, under them. Some stalled in front of them, only to move away just as they were about to collide.

'What the fuck is happening?' Zonshine shouted on his radio as the saucers started to circle the two squadrons. They spun horizontally and vertically, whirled into a spiral and then began to close in. The pilots opened fire, but the saucers were evasive and swifter than the within-visual-range missiles.

Suddenly, a voice boomed on all their radios at once: 'Reduce speed to 180 knots. Follow the flying saucers. They will guide you to your destination.'

'This is Admiral Limpdick, Commander, Joint World Island–Republic Naval Task Force. Identify yourself.'

'Captain Indra Lal Roy, No. 40 Fighter Squadron, Royal Flying Corps, accompanied by Sardar Hardit Singh Malik, No. 28 Fighter Squadron, RFC. I'm flying an SE5, and Hardit a Bristol F2. Zonshine can pick us up at ten o'clock and two o'clock. We don't want to harm your boys. We're guiding them to a landing strip as we speak. Goodbye, Admiral, have a good evening.'

Zonshine and Corey saw two First World War biplane fighters flying outside the ring of the flying saucers. The World Island pilots watched in disbelief. They had no choice but to follow the saucers.

They had been over land, they figured out, for a while.

'Drop altitude and prepare for landing,' Captain Roy's voice sounded again.

'Do as instructed,' ordered Zonshine.

The pilots could see nothing below. It was pitch dark.

'Where are we landing?' said Corey into the radio, 'We can't see a thing.'

'Don't worry, the flying saucers will show you the way. There are three runways. Split up accordingly.'

The two biplanes slowly descended, and the flying saucers jetted out in front to form three lines. By their light, Limpdick's men spotted the runways, very long ones. Soon, the F-35s began to land, three planes at a time, as the rest hovered over the airfield escorted by the saucers.

Alighting from their planes, the aviators found themselves in a derelict air base in the middle of a dense forest. The saucers had disappeared and there was no light, save for the torches they brought out of their survival kits. Since they had landed on different runways, they signalled to their companions to come together. When they were more or less all in a group, Zonshine and Corey saw the silhouettes of two men approach them. One of them wore a turban, the other an old-school flying beret.

The beret man, a very good-looking man, came up to Zonshine and shook his hand. 'Captain Indra Lal Roy. No matter what you think of Bach, Zonshine—Mahler is the best.'

Zonshine could barely speak. 'Those planes and those UFOs . . .'

'Those are fine planes, Zonshine. I downed 10 German planes flying that lady in 1918.'

The aviators gaped. Zonshine suddenly realized how cold the hand was that was still holding his own.

'Don't be spooked, Zonshine. We're all fighter pilots here. I was shot down over Carvin in France, and lie buried in Estevelles Communal Cemetery at Pas-de-Calais. I was 19. You see Hardit there? Six kills.'

The turbaned man was waving at five military trucks that had in the meantime roared down the run way and drawn to a halt a few feet away. A company of PRC soldiers jumped out, and rounded up Zonshine, Corey and their men, gesturing at them to get into the trucks.

One of them turned to Captain Roy and Sardar Singh. 'Captain Roy and Lieutenant Singh, I presume.'

'Yes,' said Roy, 'How are you doing, young man?'

'We'll leave these planes in your able hands, gentlemen. General Firebrand and General Bahadur send you their regards.'

Captain Roy nodded and moved closer to Zonshine. 'This base was used in the Second World War for B-24 and B-25 sorties against the Japs. Later, even the famed B-29s took off from here to bomb Tojo's men in Burma, Ceylon, Thailand and beyond. Yours marks the first landing since the end of the war. I thought we should part on an anecdotal note, Zonshine. We will meet again.' Zonshine looked at Captain Roy for a few moments. Then walked away and climbed into the truck. The vehicles vroomed off and were soon out of sight.

In the heart of the darkness stood forty of the most modern fighter aircraft known to mankind, and two biplanes and the spirits of two pilots who had duelled with the likes of Red Baron Manfred Von Richthofen in the First World War. The only living things were the mosquitoes and the crickets whose chirping filled the air heavy with the smell of mud.

'An era has passed in darkness and silence, Laddie,' spoke the man in the turban.

'Yes, Hobgoblin. It's time to wake up the men of honour from their sleep.'

'First let's get ourselves a drink or two. What will you have?'

'Gin and tonic. With so many mosquitoes around, the quinine should do us good.'

'The mosquitoes can't bite us any longer, Laddie.'

'I know. But when you asked me, a few of them were buzzing about my ears. It's a situational response, you see. Let's hit the officer's mess, Hobgoblin.'

The two spirits began to walk, side by side. Soon, their silhouettes melted into the dense foliage of the jungle.

XII

'Rebels Claim Capture of World Island Spy,' screamed the headlines of the *Republic Times* the next morning. International dailies like the *Guard of Europe* and *WI Post* printed a photograph of Purple Backpack on their front pages. The video of a battered and bruised Purple Backpack confessing to smuggling in a bomb to blow up Calcutta had already gone viral, with over 500 million views in just 24 hours.

The world also came to know Purple Backpack's real name.

The Office of President Adam Bum and the World Island government posted denials on their websites: they had nothing to do with any such individual; that they were committed to no first use of any weapons of mass destruction; and these were all trumped-up charges, levelled by a weakening and desperate secessionist regime.

Purple Backpack had known this would happen in case he was caught. The agency and the government wash their hands off anyone whose cover is blown. That was well understood by everyone who took part in the trade. But he truly had no clue about the contents in the lower part of the lunch box. He had used the upper part to store his meals; it had a very effective heat-retaining mechanism. He had been told not to think about the weight of the empty box. He had also been told to wait for further instructions about what to do with it. 'If and when the time is right, we'll let you know,' had been the exact words of his handler, Jonathan Bannister. Though even Jonathan had no clue about the box—that information was way above his pay grade.

Upon his arrest, the lunch box had been sent to the technical team, comprising scientists allied with the rebels. They dismantled the shell, and while they understood that within it lay a complicated nuclear device, they could not zero in on its type and specifications, nor did they have the requisite infrastructure. Consequently, a word was ferried across to the Eurasians who flew a special team into Sands, allegedly to study the human rights situation on the ground. They arrived in two strategic heavy-lift aircraft full of equipment and set up a makeshift lab inside the compound.

Eventually, it was declared to be a highly developed and miniaturized version of the neutron bomb, the programme for which had been discontinued in the 1980s and the last one known to mankind retired in 2011.

Such bombs release a large number of neutrons instead of the heat and blast power of typical thermonuclear weapons. They kill living beings instantly but are not that destructive of property and infrastructure beyond an extremely close radius. Since neutrons disappear from the atmosphere quickly, the area thus 'sanitized' can be immediately reoccupied and repopulated.

The scientists had described it to Bum as 'the ultimate capitalist bomb'. Bum had loved the idea. He had called Nida Dodi the same night and told her all about it: 'Now, we will rule the world.'

Nida had loved the idea too. She could depopulate a city, repopulate it with her own people and use its industrial infrastructure to resume production in a matter of days. 'Honestly, we should use Calcutta and Greater Calcutta as a test bed. Those roaches deserve to be roasted, Adam.'

'Let's just say we'll keep that option open, my dear.'

Brigadier Maria drove up to the command HQ of PRC Guerrillas' 1st Strike Corps that same day and stopped in front of the two-room cottage that served as Firebrand's living quarters. Although Firebrand barely used the place; most nights he spent in the dugouts with his colonels, majors, captains and foot soldiers, especially when the shelling across the river was intense.

The soldiers had never seen a General leading an assault team before. So when Firebrand led a team of 99 special-force personnel across the river to destroy the four giant guns that had been brought in by train to blow the PRC defences to smithereens, they were galvanized into action. He returned from the mission with 90 men. Both General Bahadur and Kapo called him to congratulate him, though Kapo had a word of caution: 'FB, not that you will listen to me but the force can't afford to lose you. Please keep that in mind. It's a request.'

But with the giant guns gone and the debacle of Operation First Flush still fresh in collective memory, the Republican Army and its World Island counterpart were not attacking Devil's Lair and the defences around it with the same gusto any more.

Maria dialled Firebrand's number. 'I'm at your place. When're you going to be back?'

'I should be in by 6.30 p.m. This is a surprise.'

Maria laughed. 'Hopefully, a pleasant one. I carried a pork shoulder with me from Calcutta and my ancient oven as well. You don't mind some roast for dinner, do you? And I'm crashing here for the night, hope that's OK?'

'Sounds like a plan.'

'Great, see you soon.'

That night, Firebrand was about to pass out on the couch after two drinks, a heavy meal and a long conversation during which he had in fact spoken very little. Maria said the bed was big enough for the two of them, but Firebrand said he'd stick to the couch.

'You don't like me, do you, FB?'

'It's not that.'

'Then?'

'I'm just not good at this, Maria.'

'Leave that to me to judge. Don't be so tense. I've never seen you relax. Come here. It'll be great, trust me.'

'Maria, I really don't think I can do this.'

'You don't find me attractive, FB. Isn't that the truth?'

'No, Maria. It's just that I can't.'

'It was a long, long time ago, FB. Don't you think it's time you moved on? Have you never heard of casual sex?'

'I gave everything away many moons ago, Maria. I've got nothing left to give. And I am not one of those who like to take without giving. The river has no water any more. Only rocks and stones. I'm an unpleasant and bitter man, Maria. I've made my peace with that. I think I'll make some coffee now. You want some?'

'Black, no sugar, please.'

Firebrand got up and put the kettle on.

'I'm not the best person to discuss how the Intelligence Department does its job. But no prisoner of war deserves to be treated like that. Don't you think so, Maria?'

'Are you talking about the spy?'

'Yes, I didn't have time to read the details today. Just caught a glimpse of a photo and the headline. The beating was way too severe. Once you've captured someone, that in my opinion is not what you do to them.'

'Not in my hands, FB. I asked nicely but he refused to cooperate. He wouldn't even tell me his real name. It was down to Ashley and his men. You don't know the brutes they are.'

'Hmm, so where is this lad from? And what was his mission?'

'He's a citizen of World Island but was born in Sands. He smuggled in something called a neutron bomb. I don't know the details but he was headed for Calcutta when he was intercepted. He was pretending to be a wildlife photographer. By the way, did you see his mother's video appeal for his release? Her only child, and she had no clue he worked with the agency. I feel bad, I admit.'

'I barely had a moment to read the headlines, Maria, let alone watch a video.' Firebrand poured hot water into the mugs, and glanced about for the jar of coffee.

'You should watch it. Just five minutes long. Search for "Laila Naqvi appeal".'

Firebrand flinched. 'Laila Naqvi?'

'That's the mother.'

'Laila Naqvi was my wife's name.'

'That would make this Ryan your son,' Maria chuckled.

Firebrand turned around in a flash and grabbed Maria's shoulders so hard that she winced. 'Show me. Right now.'

Gently shaking herself free, she said: 'Hang on. Give me a minute.' She picked up her cell phone and searched for and located the video. As it began to play, Firebrand almost snatched the phone out of her hands. Though she showed no sign of it, Maria was a little frightened. She'd heard about his struggle with alcohol-induced violence, and feared he might be having one such episode now.

Firebrand watched the video for just 30 seconds. Then gave the phone back to Maria, held her head gently but firmly and said, 'I'm sorry if I've hurt you. But I have to go now. I have to save my son.'

Maria stood there, frozen in shock, as Firebrand went into his room and changed his clothes. Then he called Brigadier Jha and Brigadier Pandey, ordered them to put the 12,000 men under their command in redeployment mode, ready for immediate travel. Then he called Colonel Abbas of the Special Forces unit and asked him to get the two battalions ready. He called his driver and asked him to come to his place right away.

Then, he dialled Kapo.

A few hours earlier, Yusuf had barged into Kapo's office and shown him the video appeal. Kapo's face grew pinched and pale. He called Brigadier General Padmanabhan at Army Intelligence HQ.

'Paddy, the boy, Ryan—he's not to be touched. Get him out of that underground hell. Give him a comfortable room with an air conditioner. Use the budget to furnish the room if you have to. Give him the best medical attention. At once. He should get the best food and the best care. And put guards inside and outside, 24x7.'

'But El Comandante, we were hoping to extract some more information out of the scumbag. We won't have to resort to third degree for much longer, I think. He'll let it all out if Ashley and the guys just walk into the room one more time.'

'Paddy, you have no clue who we have on our hands. And what's about to happen any minute now. Do as I say. No one should interrogate the boy any further. I want a report on his condition right away. I'm sending two men to be posted there.'

'But, El Comandante . . .'

Kapo cut him short. 'Paddy, I was there when this boy was born. This is between you and me and does not leave the room: he is General Firebrand's only child. You understand the gravity of the matter, now?'

'My God!'

'I'm on my way to Calcutta. If FB gets there before me, do not provoke him at any cost. Do whatever he wants. Just do not release the boy before I arrive. Keep FB engaged.'

'All right, El Comandante. Should I let Comrade Firebrand meet the boy?'

'You think he's going to take your permission, Paddy?'

'If Comrade Firebrand arrives with his troops, how will I stop him from taking his son away?'

'I've already asked General Salman to deploy the 2nd Reserve Army. Though nothing can stop FB from doing what he wants to do. Keep the doctors there, Paddy. Buy some time till I arrive.'

Kapo put down the phone. And got ready to leave for Calcutta at once. In the car, he found himself constantly looking at his phone, expecting Firebrand's name to flash on the screen. It finally did, at 10.30 p.m.

Kapo showed the screen to Yusuf, picked up the call and put it on speaker.

XIII

'Hello, FB. Tell me, what's happening?'

'Cut the crap, Kapo. You know why I'm calling.'

'What do you want us to do?'

'I want him taken out of that hellhole. I want doctors to treat him. No one's to touch him, Kapo.'

'I've already ensured that, Kapo. You think Ryan's uncle would not do that? As soon as I saw Laila's appeal, he was shifted to a room furnished with every comfort. The best doctors, the best meals, the best care, you name it. They're treating him like a king.'

'I'm on my way to Army Intel HQ. Once I get there, I'm taking my son out. I expect not to meet any resistance.'

'FB, calm down. I know it's difficult, but just take a moment. What will the soldiers think if you arrive in our capital with your men and take your son away like this? What will it do to the morale of the forces?'

'Kapo, I am going to take my son out of there. My men don't mean any trouble. Tell Ashley and his henchmen to get the hell out of there before I do. If I see them, I'm going to bury them alive. Are you with me or against me, Kapo?'

'I'm on my way, FB. Wait for me to get there before you do something stupid. We'll find a way to get him out.'

Firebrand disconnected and lit a cigarette. His jeep roared towards Calcutta, at the head of a huge military convoy of 14,000 of the PRC Guerrillas' toughest and most battle-hardened men.

'He's all right,' he said to Maria, sitting beside him, rigid with tension. 'Kapo got him out of the hole. He's in good care.'

'El Comandante knew?'

'He must have seen Laila's appeal. Ryan used to call him Uncle Longbeard. They played chess together. The last time they met, it was Ryan's 12th birthday. Kapo gifted him a set of Mastermind.'

'El Comandante knew your wife too?'

'Yes, he came home often.'

'I guess that should make things easier.'

'I hope it does.'

Purple Backpack—we will call him Ryan henceforth—was lying on the floor, every part of his body throbbing with pain, when he heard a commotion outside the door. Then suddenly it was flung open, and seven or eight men rushed in with a stretcher. Two wore stethoscopes around their necks. There was a nurse too.

'Hello, son, I'm Brigadier General Padmanabhan. We're shifting you someplace else, someplace you can be much more comfortable.'

Ryan's hands were untied. He was transferred onto the stretcher, and then carried out of the dungeon, up a flight of stairs. Another door. The guards outside opened it, and Ryan felt a blast of cool air sweep over him. He was carried into the air-conditioned room, with a brand-new wrought-iron bed. The whole place reeked of fresh paint; the walls were hung with Degas and Van Gogh prints. He glimpsed an attached bath as well.

The room had large windows.

The doctors dressed the wounds around his eyes, cheeks, mouth and nose. They instructed the nurse about his medicines. A machine was wheeled in, and he was gently turned this side and that so that he could be X-rayed.

'Anything serious, doctors?' asked the elderly man being referred to as General Paddy.

'The facial bruises will heal fast, General. No signs of concussions or internal bleeding. A few broken ribs. They will heal in about six weeks. He needs rest now. In case he feels dizzy and nauseous, he should be rushed to a hospital.'

'Thank god. You take care, son. Ask for anything you need.'

They slowly walked out and shut the door softly behind them. Only the nurse remained, sitting in a corner.

Ryan slowly sat up, hung his feet over the edge of the bed and discovered a pair of slippers left there for him. Sliding them on, he said to the nurse: 'Can I open the windows for a bit?'

'Of course. Let me do that for you. The paint is still raw.'

He walked over to the window and looked out at the few stars splattered above, his first sight of the sky in days. The moon had hidden itself behind the clouds. Insects buzzed around the lamp heads. The sky wore a reddish hue, almost reflecting the red-brick Victorian structures around the square. There were small puddles here and there. Beyond the high wall and the barbed-wire fence of the site where he was being held, he could see frenetic activity: military trucks arriving, troops getting down and taking up defensive positions. He could see them do the same atop the buildings around the square. Heavy machine guns, small field-artillery pieces, mortars and gunny sacks being brought in.

He wondered what had prompted this 180-degree turn on the part of his captors. Have the combined force of the Republic and World Island broken through their defences? But that seemed improbable. He studied the walls of the compound, the watchtowers and the sentry movements inside the premises. The security looked pretty tight. He knew he would take weeks to get back his usual strength. Right now, a bid to escape meant sure death. He had no choice but to wait.

Paddy walked into the room a little later. Ryan turned.

'I got you some books in case you want to read.'

'Thanks. I just want to make a phone call.'

'I have to ask for permission to let you. And I need to know whom you want to call.'

'My mother. It will be a long-distance call.'

'Let me get back to you on that, son.' Paddy left.

Ryan sat on the bed and went through the pile of books Paddy had brought him. He picked up *All the Names* by José Saramago and lay down. A few hours later, just as he was about to sink into a deep sleep—it must have been about two in the morning—the silence was broken by the sound of heavy trucks pulling up in the square outside. Then the sound of military boots hitting the ground, the cocking of weapons, the shouting of orders . . . He got up and rushed over to the window—thousands of troops in combat fatigues were streaming out of the trucks and taking up positions against the building and its walls and wire fences.

The soldiers who had got into the defensive positions earlier that evening seemed tense. He could see some of them move to the rooftops; the troops who had dug in earlier were now leaving their positions.

'Move away from the window, son,' Paddy shouted from the door and rushed off.

'What's happening?' Ryan shouted and raced back to the bed. Would he be safer in the underground room?

Paddy called General Salman. 'Where are you? Comrade Firebrand's men are taking over the square. They're threatening your men. Your boys are chickening out.'

'I'm right here. Can you see FB?'

'No, I can't. I can see the special units sanitizing the rooftops. Tell your men to grow some balls. They're shitting in their pants at the mere look of these chaps from 1st Strike Corps.'

'It's just a reserve army, Paddy. I don't blame them. I've told them not to provoke FB's men in any way. Those are my orders, and I have to follow them.'

'Salman, I'm at the foot of the monument in the square. Get down here.'

General Salman arrived a few moments later, huffing and puffing. 'Paddy, is the boy doing fine?'

'Yes, he was reading and resting even half an hour ago.'

Paddy pulled out his phone and called Firebrand. 'Hello, Comrade Firebrand. General Salman and I are waiting for you under the martyrs' monument.'

'Paddy, I'll be there in five minutes.'

Firebrand disconnected as Maria got out of the car. 'I'll see you later, Maria. This is my shit. No one else gets into trouble for it.'

'You know what, FB? You're not as badass as you like to pretend. Go, do what you have to do.'

Firebrand's car revved off in the direction of the Army Intelligence HQ and, four minutes later, entered the square followed by two trucks carrying 90 of the PRC Guerrillas' finest killing machines. Their combat fatigues were distinct. The men rolled out of their trucks and in a few seconds assumed their positions.

Firebrand got out of the car, and shook hands with Paddy and Salman. 'My men and I mean no harm, comrades. Only these 90 will enter with me.'

'Sure thing, FB,' said General Salman. 'Paddy, you got no issues with that, right?'

'Absolutely not. I've kept the doctors waiting too in case Comrade Firebrand wants to speak to them.'

'That's good,' said Firebrand, striding down the square at the head of the 90 lean and mean men. Once inside, the men spread around, covering the courtyard, the staircases, the corridors. Only 10 among them accompanied Firebrand up to the room. Paddy was about to open the door when Firebrand said, 'Paddy, give me a minute. If you don't mind, I'd like some time alone with him.'

'Of course, Comrade Firebrand. I'll request the nurse to leave the room,' Paddy smiled and held the door open.

A gust of chilled air billowed out and swept over Firebrand. Its cold fingers ruffled his beard, but Firebrand didn't flinch.

XIV

President Adam Bum walked into the meeting almost half an hour before the PRC press conference involving the captured World Island pilots was scheduled to begin.

His Secretary of State Frank Pollard, Defence Secretary Shane Fairbanks and Director of the intelligence agency Elizabeth Horowitz wore nervous smiles as Mr President took his place at the head of the table.

'This has been annoying me a bit, you know. But I guess there was no other way to deal with Limpdick.'

'You did the right thing, Mr President,' Shane said, 'You cannot have a deranged person in charge of men and ships and a war.'

'It's just that his background is so solid. His role in Iraq was exemplary.'

'I don't honestly know about that, Bummer,' Frank said, fiddling with a pen, 'The disappearance of all those weapons, the use of Second World War sniper bullets and now a career Admiral spouting gibberish. There is a method to this . . . we just don't know what it is.'

'Hmmm . . . Liz, what are we doing to retrieve the Lunch Box?'

'We're working on it, Mr President. They've moved it from the lab. We have a few leads. Once we zero in on a location, we'll send in a team.'

'We have to move fast. Dodi is driving me crazy. She's convinced they'll detonate it in her capital.'

'We're doing our best, Mr President. Let me just say that the Republic's intelligence inputs on this matter have been sketchy at best. We will also try and extract our operative, bring him back home.'

'There is an ongoing campaign for his release,' Frank said, 'His mother's travelling there. His release will be a big shot in your arm, Bummer.'

'It's time,' said Shane, switching on the big monitor in front of them.

'Those are Lieutenant Commanders Daniel Zonshine and Tinpot Corey, Mr President,' Shane said as the television image zeroed in on two men seated at a table. In front of them were a clutch of microphones, arranged like a bouquet.

The press conference had begun.

'Is it true that your planes were shot down by the PRC air-defence batteries?'

'We were not shot down. We were force-landed. The adversary sent in flying saucers led by two Royal Flying Corps fighter pilots.'

'Flying saucers?' some of the reporters hooted with laughter.

'Yes, flying saucers, discs, some large, some small, spinning at great speed. We were shooting at them but they evaded fire. Then they created a ring around us and forced us to land in an airbase last used in the Second World War.'

'What are you chaps smoking?' shouted a French TV reporter.

'Nothing. This is for real. Have a word with Admiral Limpdick's office. He spoke to their pilot over the radio. I'm forgetting the name of the one of the aviators in charge of this forced landing, but he claimed he had 10 Luftwaffe kills in 1918.'

'Captain Indra Lal Roy,' said the turbaned man who had just walked in through the door at the back. As Lieutenant Hardit Singh Malik—or the Flying Hobgoblin, according to his nick—walked up to Zonshine and Corey's table, the press took note of his antiquated pilot suit. The cameras went crazy. 'He was shot down in France in 1918,' Hobgoblin said, as he walked over to Zonshine, and then leant into the microphones: 'If you train your cameras through the windows, you'll be able to see Laddie. That's what we used to call Captain Roy in the RFC. He's leading a flypast of the captured planes.'

The assembled press watched agape as Captain Indra Lal Roy appeared in his SE5 and waved at them, followed by 40 F-35s in 8–5 arrowhead formations. An unmanned Bristol F-2 biplane hovered by the window. Hobgoblin jumped into the cockpit, pulled down the canopy and zoomed off to join his colleagues in the sky.

Frank switched off the monitor and the four of them sat in silence for a while.

Shane's phone buzzed.

'Hello.'

'Sir, Admiral Townsend has just sent in some forensic reports from Admiral Limpdick's quarters.'

'And?'

'The strands of hair found in his room do belong to a large feline, sir—it's jaguar DNA.'

'Anything else?'

'No, sir.'

Shane put the phone down and turned towards the President. 'Mr President, it looks like Admiral Limpdick was not hallucinating. They ran forensics. There was indeed a large wild cat in his room. They tested the hairs and found out.'

Again, a long silence. Then Bum finally spoke. 'What are we up against here, Frank? A wild cat in the middle of the ocean? And if they can take 40 F-35s under their control, they can take control of our fleet as well. Whatever Limpdick said is turning out to be true. Should we pull out while there's time?'

'I don't think we can pull out after this press conference. The world will laugh at us. The Eurasians will think we've got no balls left any more. And what about our other alliance partners? If we fail to come to Republic's defence, we are failing them. It'll be the end of the Coalition of the Righteous.'

'What the hell have we got ourselves into?'

'I think the mess will do your re-election bid good. We love our military to get embroiled in shit,' Shane said.

He was right. Most people in the world do get turned on by the sight of their air force pounding people to dust 10,000 kilometres away. A songwriter once described it as 'the bravery of being out of range'. But as far as jingoism went, World Island was a class apart. No other people could make better puppets in the hands of the masters of war.

'But what if the shit really does hit the fan?' Bum was worried. His realty company's stocks were not doing well at all since these strange events had begun to occur.

'Then we run, men and boys alike,' Frank said with a smile, much to the annoyance of Liz. She had always found this trio utterly misogynistic, three sexist dogs she had no choice but to work alongside.

A fly had been buzzing around the table for a while now. Fed up, Bum rolled up one of the reports in front of him and then swatted it dead with so much force, the table shuddered and creaked in protest.

'It looks like we're stuck. Liz, we have to get the Lunch Box back. And what about the lad?'

'He's in their custody. His mother's flying out tonight to secure his release.'

'Godspeed to her. If she can pull it off, it'll be nothing short of a miracle. I'll give him a President's Medal and you can give him a desk job. We can't do more.'

'There've been some murmurs in the agency that we should conduct a rescue op. But I've made it clear that we don't do that. We're not the military. We do leave people behind. I don't want to set a precedent.'

'That's why I love you, Liz. You always get things under control. I've got a meeting with the Saudi king now. Class dismissed,' Bum laughed, terribly pleased at his own wit. Liz found his laughter getting louder by the day. He must be growing more nervous, she thought.

The two men and the woman left. Bum went to the washroom to freshen up. Then he called Nancy, his latest pin-up model muse, and set up a post-dinner rendezvous at her apartment. He felt slightly better. He badly needed a boost before getting down to negotiating oil contracts. He checked the stock price of Bum Realty. 'Shit, fucking red again!'

Twenty-four hours later, a special aircraft carrying Laila Naqvi landed in Calcutta. In the absence of flight operations between Tantilash and Calcutta, it required special clearance from PRC. The clearance had come within five minutes of the Republican authorities putting in their request.

XV

When Aurelio and Sitaram emerged from Olga's hut for the steep trek to their den in the Island of Bald Mountain, dawn had just started to break. The first rays of the sun, trapped overnight in a box of darkness, could not hide their childlike haste; they rushed out and scattered all over the waters. As they crossed the ocean, they seemed to panic that they were going astray; so they came together a few moments later on a black stone embedded at the foot of the tallest peak, overlooking the range. On top of it, inside the crater, lay the Hollow, the den of Aurelio the Shaman and Sitaram the Tantric.

From afar, the volcano looked like a giant dark-brown phallus. Inside, the mirror-glossy walls of white quartzite, green olivine and reddish feldspar bounced the rays of the sun off each other in a seemingly endless game of colourful catch. At night, the game played on, then reflecting the glow of the wood fires that Aurelio and Sitaram would light.

There were other fires too. One for cooking, and several others for the strange rituals that the duo conducted. Occasionally, people from the forest villages came with their requests: to ask their dead ancestors for advice about their crop failures and forest fires, about settling sibling disputes and domestic troubles. They paid in kind, with grains, vegetables, oil, clothes, firewood, earthen utensils, tobacco, fermented-date alcohol and cannabis. At times, even a duck or a goat. Their gifts helped Aurelio and Sitaram survive. Since their rickety boat had landed on the green lagoon's shore two and a half years ago, they had settled in well.

Olga the Whore, the third occupant of the boat, had stayed with them for some time before setting up her own hut at the foot of the last hillock next to the forest. She lived there with her pet Sloth Bear, Blind Hyena and her pack of hunting dogs. Living close to the forest worked out well for Olga—close enough for the men from the villages to visit, far enough for their assignations to be somewhat discreet.

Occasionally, Olga would visit the Hollow with vegetables from her garden or with a jungle fowl her dogs had hunted. The three would cook up a meal. Sometimes Aurelio and Sitaram came to her hut. Aurelio had grown fond of the bear, and Sitaram of the hyena. They would sing songs of Los Jairas and Alla Pugacheva. Sitaram would throw in the occasional bhajan and play the bamboo flute.

But that night, there were no songs. Talking Crane had informed them about the meeting at Olga's hut. The three of them were in place well before time. On the stroke of midnight, Marshal Georgy Zhukov walked in. He had a friend with him, dressed in a blue brocade overcoat. This bearded stranger could tell by their expressions that they were intrigued by his garb.

'This is a deel. It's what Mongol kings wore, except when we went to war. And since we went to war almost all the time, I am making up for all that lost opportunity,' he laughed childishly, baring his teeth and gums.

'Meet my friend Khan,' said Zhukov. And then proceeded to give them clear instructions: 'In three days, it will be two full months since the day the long-horned bird ended her life. On the fourth day, at 1.15 a.m., when the moon goes into hiding, the Great Pull must begin. So, from tomorrow, you need to get into action.'

'We are ready,' said Sitaram. 'What about the list of things that we handed over to Talking Crane?'

'When you return to the Hollow tomorrow morning, you will find three bags,' said Khan.

'The map too, with the markings?' asked Sitaram.

'Yes, no misses there, Guruji,' laughed Zhukov.

Sitaram turned towards Aurelio and Olga and stretched out his palm. 'Let's do it. It is time.'

The two put their hands on top of Sitaram's, and the Marshal of the Soviet Union in the Great Patriotic War and Khan placed a hand each on top of theirs. 'Let's do this.'

They finished three pitchers of date wine in silence, and then the two guests took their leave. It was almost morning. When Aurelio and Sitaram stepped out, they could see the colony of bats heading back to their caves in the mountain from the forests. Their feeding time was over. Soon, the birds would come out. The villagers would wake up, shit, eat and get down to their chores. They lay down on the wet grass for a few minutes, soaking in the sight of the sky, the sounds of the bird-songs before they started walking back to their lair.

'I'll go spearfishing after lunch. We've been having too much meat of late,' said Aurelio as they began to climb the mountain. If you saw them from afar, you would think they were mountain goats. But even at their speed, getting to the top would take at least 20 minutes.

'I'll come with you. I haven't had a salt-water swim since the rains began. I have to collect the clay too. But you have to give it the proper shape, you're good at making models.'

'If building sand castles counts. But whatever you say, Guruji.'

'Have you seen the sky? It's going to rain again.'

'It means the big fish will come near the shore. Good, saves us trouble.'

'Maybe we should take the boat and go a little deeper. The water there is so tranquil. When you float there and stare into the sky—it's magic, it's heaven.'

'Sitaram, that's not a good idea at all. That's where the shark took Channa's son on the full moon.'

'Is that so? I thought those boys had gone beyond the rock. In that case, let's stick close to shore.'

Once they entered the crater and climbed down the steps, they could see three large jute bags stacked in a corner, their mouths tied tightly with string. Villagers from Ropa, led by Elan, the headman, soon came in and began to unload firewood in one of the three caves that branched out of the inner sanctum. Ever since Aurelio had revived Elan's from a poisonous snakebite two years ago, the men of Ropa came every fortnight and replenished their firewood supply. Sitaram and Aurelio always kept the fires burning. Even when the skies opened up and rainwater poured in incessantly through the mouth of the crater, they would have at least one fire burning in their sleep corner, beneath a rocky protrusion that acted as a roof.

'How are you, Elan?' asked Aurelio.

'It's been good this far. I just hope the sky does not shed more tears than the land can hold. Then we will have to weep too.'

'It won't,' said Sitaram. 'You will have a good harvest. By the way, the rope at the well is giving in. Could you bring us a new one?'

'I'll have it done before sundown.'

'We may be out.'

'Not a problem.'

'Could you call a meeting of all the village headmen three days from now? We have something important to share. Things are going to happen. Villagers need to know. It will be an evening meeting.'

'I'll send the word out today. Evening should not be a problem. Will it be here?'

'Yes, or better, at Olga's. That will be closer for all of you.'

'Yes, it will save some of us the climb. We'll be off now. The things that will happen . . . you said . . . they will be good things?'

'Different things. I wish I knew more. Godspeed, Elan.'

Sitaram and Aurelio opened the bags and emptied them of their contents. It took them about 20 minutes to sort and settle everything. Once they were satisfied, they went out fishing. Sitaram took one of the empty bags with him.

Around 40 minutes later, they finally arrived at the white sands by the green lagoon. The walk had been worth it. In half an hour, Aurelio managed to spear a large kingfish. Sitaram swam for a while. On the way back, it began to rain. Sitaram stopped here and there, and filled the bag with clay and small stones.

'Bring Olga, Aurelio. She loves kingfish.'

'Yes, Guruji, I'll go and fetch her. You can clean the fish.'

They resumed their trek back to the Hollow, the kingfish slung over Aurelio's shoulder. The sky was a shade darker. The rain heavier, the raindrops larger.

'How bored must the Bald Mountain be,' mused Sitaram as he looked up.

'Yes, it must be painful to stand still for so long.'

Under the dark sky, the mountain stood as a stoic witness to the timeless ebb and flow of the waters that surrounded the island. While the mounds strewn across the plains wore coats of moss and shrubs, nothing ever grew on the gargantuan brown structure of volcanic rock. That's why the villagers called it the Bald Mountain.

XVI

Once every three months, Madame President would take an evening off. She'd come home by three, and switch off her phone. No calls were let through by the operators to her residence until eight the next morning. Not even Bum's.

The routine that day was no different from the one 90 days before that. She got home, changed into pyjamas and T-shirt and went into the kitchen. Her two helpers had already cut the vegetables, the fish and the meat as per as her instructions. The lentils and the rice were well soaked, the spices and condiments kept ready in small bowls.

By the time she emerged from the kitchen at six, she had cooked up a seven-course meal. She was happy, all the dishes had turned out exactly right. As she lay in the bathtub, she softly sang a traditional wedding folk song in her mother tongue. Her mother used to sing it beautifully, and Nida had inherited her golden voice. She had wanted to be a singer at one point of time. She could not remember when. Or perhaps she did not want to remember. At the monastery, she had been taught only to remember important things. And Nida had always been a keen learner.

After her bath, she spent a long time getting dressed. When she was done, she was wearing a bridal dress, heavy gold ornaments and even heavier make-up. Then she went to the dining hall and made sure the table was well laid out, that nothing was out of place. Then she put on some music and sat in the veranda that ran along the rectangular room.

About half an hour later, a rather nondescript man in a deadman shirt, dirty rubber slippers and terrycloth trousers was ushered into the house through the back gate. The perimeter lights were off, and the security guard had been waiting for the knock on the door hidden behind the hedgerow.

Many of you may not be aware of deadman shirts. And those who are, they do not buy deadman clothes anyway. These are clothes taken off corpses and then sold on the streets at throwaway prices. Similarly, there are deadman shoes, deadman belts, deadman undergarments, deadman socks, deadman sarees, deadman skirts . . . Now, don't ask me why they are not called deadwoman sarees or deadwoman skirts. Everything in this world does not follow good sense. Actually, almost nothing does, not even our minds. And even if you have the most sorted head on your shoulders, the world outside cares two hoots for it. The universe gets more disorganized as it gets older. That's just how it is. The entropy of the universe forms the second law of thermodynamics.

The frail figure climbed up the carpeted stairs to the veranda on the first floor. Madame President beamed as their eyes met. 'You must be tired. Let's go inside.'

'How are you? I've been reading everything the newspapers have been writing about you. I can't help but worry.'

'It's OK. I've decided to let them write a bit nowadays. Helps them release pressure. You must be hungry. Come, dinner is ready.'

The man left his slippers on the veranda, wore the clean pair kept in a corner and followed Madame President into the house, straight to the bathroom. When he came out 15 minutes later, he had showered and put on a polka-dot sleeping suit. 'I'm famished, I must admit.'

Madame President served the food herself. She stood beside him and waited for the long 40 minutes he took to run through the seven courses. Once he was done with the cottage-cheese dessert, he proceeded to wash his hands and mouth. Nida Dodi waited there too, with a towel in her hand.

'It wasn't very good, I know. Especially the lamb.'

'It was wonderful. It was perfect. Now it's your turn to eat.'

While Madame President ate, and she barely ate at all, the man went back to the bedroom and lay down on the king-size bed. Nida Dodi walked in a few minutes later and lay beside him with a palm-leaf fan in her hand. Her hand did not stop waving the fan even for a minute. When it did slow down and finally stop, the room was already resonating with snores.

Nida Dodi and her mystery man had never made love. That day was no exception. Their romance was strictly asexual. And that's how they both wanted it. Nobody knew where they had met, how the most powerful woman on the planet could fall for a man who ran a tiny electronics repair shop in a working-class neighbourhood on the fringes of Tantilash. No one barring five people in the Republic knew about him. And they were intelligent enough to not open their mouths.

The duo was jolted awake by an intense rocking of the bed. Nida lit her bedside lamp and saw the ceiling lights swinging from side to side. All her beautiful curios and showpieces were sliding off the mantle and crashing to the floor. 'Earthquake,' she screamed. They ran out onto the front lawns where soon they were joined by the maids and security guards.

The tremors lasted for quite some time.

About 1,800 kilometres away, Laila Naqvi and Ryan were also fast asleep when the ground beneath them began to shake. Laila had arrived that morning. As soon as she stepped out onto the tarmac, she was whisked away to the Le Grande Hotel in the city's Esplanade area. It was one of the few remaining hotels in Calcutta that were still functional. Ever since Sands had declared its independence and civil war had erupted four years ago, tourism and business had both taken a hit. Many hotel chains headquartered in Davnagar, Tantilash and beyond had slowly shut shop. Le Grande was reduced to a shadow of its opulent past. Still, it was the best that Calcutta could offer. Ryan had been shifted there the morning Firebrand had arrived at the PRC Intelligence HQ. It had been El Comandante's decision.

Laila had never thought she would be back in this city. And what a strange circumstance had brought about this visit, she thought, as the military vehicle cut across the maddening city traffic. She had not visited her hometown even when her parents died eight years ago in quick succession. Laila had always known that if one of them died, the other would be quick to follow. She wrote to her sister after her father's death: 'If one leaves, who does the other fight with? And without fighting, how could have they lived?'

Laila had always hated Calcutta. The city had never been good to her. She had almost no happy memories of it. Her childhood, when she had not been in school or asleep in bed, had been spent on the water tank on the terrace of their old house. It was the only place where she could read without being distracted by the fights between her parents. As an adult, meeting Ryan's father, then having Ryan and being a family for those first 10 years . . . that had been good. It had made her happy. After 10 years, of course, even that had been swept away by a flood of alcohol, rage, violence and blackouts.

The bombed-out buildings lining the streets stared at her with their hollow eyes and metal teeth. At one point, as the car stopped at a red light, Laila looked out and spotted Mandarin, the Chinese restaurant. This was where, almost three decades ago, she'd been riding pillion on her would-be husband's rickety Enfield motorcycle and a car had come along and hit them. She still remembered the shocked look on his face, how they'd crawled over to the side of the road somehow. Luckily, apart from a few scrapes and bruises, they had sustained no serious injuries.

The floodgates had been flung open. Despite her best intentions, the memories were rushing back . . .

Ryan knew his mother was on her way but not when exactly she would arrive. As she walked in and sat beside him on the bed, he rolled over and put his hands around her. Laila held him close. 'Don't worry son. We'll be out of here in a jiffy.'

'I'm not worried, Mamma. They're treating me quite well. But it's good to see you.'

'Somebody's being brave here.'

'It's not that, Mamma. First, Dad takes me out of the hell-hole, puts me up in this place and then you arrive. It feels strange, you know. Just like old times.'

'Dad! Where did he appear from?'

'It's a long story, Mamma.'

For the next half hour, Laila listened to Ryan with rapt attention. Since Firebrand had not spoken much during his interactions with Ryan, most of it had been pieced together from what he'd heard from Uncle Longbeard and Paddy and Maria and the guards assigned to him.

'He's changed completely. He barely speaks.'

'Ummm . . . Did he ask about me? Not that it matters . . . '

'Not much. I guess he didn't have to. I filled him up with the details pretty good.'

'I guess if he was even remotely concerned, he wouldn't have fallen off the grid like that. He just disappeared. Didn't even check his email.'

'Uncle Longbeard told me he did that so as to not endanger you or me. He said any digital footprint linking him to us would have been dangerous for us. He's right, Mamma. I would never have landed a job at the agency and you would have faced long hours of grilling if they discovered our links to a PRC Guerrilla commander.'

'And that's coming from Kapo, his partner in crime. He'll defend your father no matter what your father does. What else did he say?'

'Not much, he really does not talk at all. I asked him if he'd been seeing someone, he said no. I asked him if his health was OK. He said yes. I asked him about the slight limp he has now. He said it's nothing. He talks in monosyllables.'

'That's not Roy at all. But, then, I guess people change.'

'I think he misses you, Mamma. And he has been fighting a real war. Seen a lot of deaths. Possibly been responsible for quite a few of them. It can't be a pleasant feeling. I spoke about you a lot. And he listened to it all so calmly. He said he was glad you were happy. He meant it. You could see it in his eyes.'

'Water under the bridge, son. We were both bad news for each other in the end.'

'You have a look on your face when I talk about him. And his eyes shone every time I took your name. It's strange that you guys were so terrible at staying together.'

'I guess so. It's not that we were all bad. We had a lot of happy times, made a lot of happy memories too. But I guess everything in this world comes with its expiry date.'

'There were bad times too, Mamma, nightmarish ones.'

'Honestly, I don't remember them any more. But yes, I do wish things had turned out differently. But that is what life is. We can't change what is done.'

'By the way, he's given up drinking.'

'Good for him.'

'Do you think you guys can give it one more shot? It's been a long time.'

'Are you mad?' Laila snapped.

'I am you and Dad put together. What else do you expect me to be?'

'That's not funny, Ryan. Not after everything we've been through.'

'I'm going out for some fresh air,' Ryan said, and reached for a pair of jeans and a shirt off the clothes rack. He was upset.

Laila slowly walked up behind him and held him close.

'I know I'm a difficult person to live with, Ryan. And I'm sorry for messing up your life.'

'What are you saying, Mamma? You've not had it easy, either. Very few women would have made it through. It's just that you guys have not moved on. Neither of you. You're still living with each other's memories.'

'We can talk about this later. Where are you going?'

'Just to get some fresh air. You freshen up and I'll be back soon.'

'Will they let you go out just like that?'

'They can't refuse General Firebrand's son. I've been exploring the city on and off for the last few days. One of the guards is an encyclopaedia on Calcutta. And I have a vehicle at my disposal, Mamma,' Ryan smiled.

'What kind of a name is Firebrand? He's always been so bad with names.'

'Mamma, it was given to him.'

'Whatever. It's a horrible name, like some all-devouring dragon. Anyway, would you mind if I join you? I just need to have a shower and then we can go out for lunch.'

'Sure.'

Nida Dodi and her mystery man went back to sleep 40 minutes or so after the tremors. They woke up early the next morning and had breakfast. At 7.30, he left by the same back gate and got into the same vehicle that had brought him over the previous evening. Before he climbed down the stairs, Nida slid a fat wad of notes into the back pocket of his trousers. They held each other briefly but exchanged no words.

Laila and Ryan had gone back to sleep after a while as well. When the quake struck, they had been swiftly escorted out by two guards and run across the street to the lawns on the other side. A fat businessman, two European journalists and some members of a wedding party ran out and joined them. The hotel sent over tea and coffee and their trademark almond cookies. Ryan took an entire plateful for himself. They were very tired.

They'd had lunch at Tung Fong on Free School Street, driven to Scoop by the Hooghly for ice-cream and then walked along the river.

'This is where your dad and I immersed your grandmother's ashes,' Laila said, pointing to a flight of steps leading down to the water. Ryan saw 'Judges Ghat' written on a plaque.

They sat down on a bench. Laila listened to the rustle of the leaves that the river breeze brought to her. Ryan could hear the music of the water splashing against the mud banks. At a distance, the last rites for some freshly departed soul were being performed. To Laila, the riverfront had always been an oasis of serenity in the middle of the indifferent and vague busyness of the city. It still was very much the same.

After a while, she spoke without taking her eyes off the water. 'Did Dad come to visit you after getting you out of prison?'

'Yes, every two or three days. He came yesterday. He said he wouldn't be able to come any more. He said the fighting had got worse. He left a bagful of things he said he wanted me to have. It's a huge bag and it's very heavy.'

'I see.' She was still staring at the water. You could see the depth of the Ganges in her deep, black eyes.

'Uncle Longbeard will come day after tomorrow. If he says yes, I'll go and pay Dad a visit. I want to say goodbye to him. I don't think I'll see him again. This war's getting bloodier by the day.'

'If that's what you want.'

'Will you come with me?'

'Should I? Will he be comfortable with it?'

'The question is whether you'll be comfortable. When are we going back?'

'Sometime next week, as soon as you can walk properly. By the way, you are going to leave the agency as soon as we get back home.'

XVII

Places on the map were marked in red to identify the geoglyphs along which the men and women of Sands had been tirelessly digging for weeks. They had dug deep, so deep that the mounds of earth dumped at a distance now formed a series of not-so-small hills in the middle of the lush green plains. Barren plateaus suddenly saw grass break out across expansive swathes. Holes had been drilled into the hundreds of thousands of iron poles that were then placed into the ground at a distance of 30 metres from the digging lines all along the perimeter of the liberated zone. Anchor ropes were put through the holes and secured as instructed by Marshal Rokossovsky.

Aurelio sat with the huge mound of clay and stone chips on one side and a large earthen frying-pan-shaped vessel in front of him. He put the map on the pan and was relieved to see that it fit nicely. After cutting away the edges with a pair of scissors, he used a nail to make perforations along the red lines. Then he took lumps of clay from the mound and laid them in the pan. Adding some stone chips, he made a dough out of it all and beat it with a rock to make it flat and fill the whole pan.

Then he called out to Olga.

Olga pressed the cut-out map down on top of the clay like a stencil. Aurelio took a knife and cut away the extra clay and then dug a red thread along the perforations, deep into the dough that was now in the shape of the landmass on the map.

Then he went to the well to clean his muddy hands as Olga walked over and sat by Sitaram who was making a pot of smoke. As Aurelio came and sat by the fire, Sitaram extended the pot towards him. 'You have worked hard, Curuji. Light the chillum.' Aurelio cut a little piece off a coconut-coir rope, tied it into a ring and tossed it into the fire. Then he took out a small piece of cloth from his pocket and wrapped it around the base of the pot. As he clasped his hands around the chillum and brought it to his mouth, Sitaram lifted the burning rope ring from the fire and put it on the top of the pot. Aurelio started working his lungs and after three controlled pulls, breathed in deeply. The pot caught flame as Aurelio closed his eyes and passed it on to Sitaram. But only after he unwrapped the cloth at the base.

Sitaram and Aurelio would never use a common smoking cloth. Olga had to use her own as well. Sharing a safi, as Sitaram called it, resulted in clash of energies and a depletion of the same. Shamans and tantrics believe that the human spit holds a lot of energy and that should never mingle with another's. It was a good smoke. The weed the villagers had got them was pure, and Sitaram would always make it with chewing tobacco. Soon, all three were happy and relaxed.

'How many minutes to go,' asked Olga. Aurelio closed his eyes for a few seconds. 'Ten.'

'OK.'

A few moments later, Sitaram began to pour water all around the clay model. Then he took a fresh small mound of clay and drew two eyes, a nose and a mouth on it, and placed it on top. Aurelio handed each of them a knife. 'On my command—now!'

The three made small cuts on their index fingers and as the blobs of red started oozing out, they brought their hands over the vessel and let the blood flow onto the lines of red thread. The model started to shake and smoke began to billow from the gaps.

'The ground shakes,' Olga exclaimed.

'Yes,' said Sitaram, 'the thrill has begun.'

The readers must have figured out by now that it was right at this moment that Madame President and her lover in Tantilash and Laila Naqvi and her son in Calcutta were woken up by the tremors.

As for Aurelio, Olga and Sitaram: they had gone off to sleep after the ritual. The next morning, they were woken up by Elan of Ropa and the heads of 33 other villages. Aurelio addressed the gathering, then Sitaram took over. Then Olga drew lines in the dust with a stick, trying to explain it all.

When all the chief's questions had been answered, and the meeting concluded, Elan came up to Aurelio. 'You are speaking the truth, Shaman?'

'Yes, Elan. Don't you trust me?'

'I do. But I am scared, for my people, for my family. I am responsible for what happens to them, Shaman.'

'It's all right, Elan. No harm will come to your people. Go with a calm mind.'

That morning, Marshal Rokossovsky paid a visit to Firebrand's cottage along with his friend Marshal Rodion Malinovsky. They discussed the front in detail, and Malinovsky gave Firebrand a daring idea for breaking through the Republican lines.

'Rodion, I don't think they can pull off a Donbas in two days,' grinned Rokossovsky.

'Oh, yes, that's true. My old mind . . . It's just that the sound of the guns gets to me like nothing else,' Malinovsky said, sipping on the black coffee Firebrand had made. The Republican forces had started shelling the ramparts by the river before sunrise, and soon the PRC guns were responding with a booming chorus of their own.

'Too few guns for our liking, Rodion.'

'Is it confirmed? The night after 48 hours?' Firebrand asked.

'Yes,' said Rokossovsky, 'but you can't tell anyone.'

'But many will die—scores will be hurt if not forewarned.'

'Who said not to warn them? Just use a different warning. That's all.'

On their way out, Malinovsky turned to Firebrand: 'You should have been there, soldier. When we opened up the Ukraine front:11,000 heavy guns, 2,000 Katyushas raining hell on the Wehrmacht. And then we pushed the bastards all the way to Berlin. All that blood and snow. The horizon was a collage of red and white. Bolshevik blood, Nazi blood, rotting bodies half-eaten by wolves, mangled heaps of metal, burnt-out farms, deserted villages, razed cities, famished people staring across the barbed-wire fence of the concentration camps, the smell of young flesh in the crematoria in Belsen, Buchenwald, Krakow, Lublin . . . the hissing of the gas valves . . . the paper-weights made out of children's heads in the SS office . . . the soaps made from human fat. That was a war we simply had to win.'

'Yes.'

'And this is a war you have to win as well, General Firebrand. Show no mercy. Give no quarter and take nothing back.'

'Yes, Marshal. To victory, always.'

'You are no longer afraid. You were, when we first met,' said Rokossovsky.

'So long, Marshals. So long.'

Over the next two days, Sitaram kept checking the water level in the earthen pan. Every night, the three made fresh cuts on their fingers and let the blood drip onto the red thread. Sitaram and Aurelio stopped eating anything but for the fruits that Olga's pet Sloth Bear gathered for them. On the third day, they stopped eating that too. But they did smoke a liberal number of chillums. They tried their best to persuade Olga to have her meals. But she would not budge.

In their spare time, Sitaram and Olga played a tiger-hunt game on an Alquerque board: two tigers attempted to elude capture and hunt as many sheep as possible while the 20 sheep attempted to corner the predators. In the absence of a proper board, they used a stick to draw patterns in the dust.

The tigers won every time even though they were outnumbered 10 to 1.

XVIII

Firebrand was not feeling too well when he came back to his cottage that night. It had been a tiring day on the front. The enemy had mounted an offensive across the river the night before and he'd had to rush to the frontline at 1.30 a.m. He heated up a little rice and lentil soup but stopped after two or three spoons, rushed to the loo and hurled it all out. As he hunched over the commode, the image of a 20-year-old boy's face being blown away kept flashing through his mind. He had just got to know the boy. Even ordered him to lie low in the trench. But, then, it was a war out there, and such things were bound to happen. All it took was a second, sometimes less.

He had been down in the trenches all day, manning a heavy machine gun and shouting orders on the radio. The enemy had set off a massive artillery bombardment before launching precision missiles at the fortified dugouts and turrets. As if he had a premonition, Firebrand had pulled the heavy artillery back two days ago, beyond the defensive perimeter: they were to camouflage themselves in the bushes some kilometres away and respond with light machine-gun and rifle fire. Once the attacking troops were on the pontoon bridge and their rafts had crossed the middle of the river, Firebrand ordered a rocket salvo from two batteries positioned 30 kilometres from the frontline. Each of the 12 launchers let off 40 rockets in a minute. After 10 minutes, the entire enemy rear-guard had been wiped out and the rockets had sanitised a 4-square-kilometre area. It was then that Firebrand ordered intensive fire on the forces on the bridge and the rafts.

As more than 100 heavy machine guns, thousands of rifles, mortars and rocket-propelled grenades rained fire on the forces in the river, the machine gunners atop the rafts also responded in kind. But soon snipers from the houses and buildings and minarets of Devil's Lair started taking them out. Firebrand was firing a PKT general-purpose machine gun. He must have fired more than 10,000 rounds himself.

Two days before the assault, Republican authorities had closed the dam upstream. Consequently, the river had very little flow. As daylight broke, one could see hundreds of bodies floating on the water like dead fish.

The assault had been a total failure.

Firebrand stepped out for a bit of air. It was late in the night. He took off his boots and walked on the grass. His feet grew wet with dew, it felt good. He lay down for a bit, clutching the wet blades in his hands. He was breathing heavily. There was a shooting pain in his chest, towards the left. It had started two days ago while he was driving back from Calcutta after seeing Ryan, and it was getting worse. He had thought of visiting the field hospital for a check-up but where was the time? He looked at the sky. It was overcast and dark. Not a star in sight. And then he fell asleep. A stray dog, white and brown, came and lay down next to him.

The next morning, he woke up late. He looked at the jet black sky. He had never seen such an apocalyptic sky. Like a massive blackboard, hung overhead. One could write on with the white clouds, he thought. He went inside and took out his ukulele from its case. It'd been so long since he'd touched it. He took off the rusty strings and cleaned it with a wet cloth, put new strings on and tuned it. He played for a while. He sang a few songs, including one he had composed when Ryan was 10. Ryan had quipped, 'This will win you the Grammy, Dad.' He smiled as he remembered. Then he made himself a strong cup of coffee and dialled El Comandante on the phone. It was almost noon.

'Hello, FB. You're good?'

'Yes, but the casualties have been heavy.'

'So I heard, but we have given them back many times.'

'Maybe. Anyway, I called for a different reason. I'm going to make an announcement on Radio Liberation. It will be a super-cyclone warning. You need to endorse it. The old, the children, the sick need to be moved into the concrete structures. We've already packed the essentials, right? Those who have sturdy houses need to stay indoors after 4 p.m.'

'FB, has the time come?'

'Yes, but this stays between us.'

'FB, Ryan and Laila have left Calcutta early this morning for your place.'

'Kapo, you have to call them back. They need to fly out before this begins.'

'There are no planes, FB. And have you seen the sky? No aircraft can land in such conditions.'

'We will see about this later then.'

'FB, stay safe, man.'

'Hmm, I'll try my best, Kapo. You too.'

As Firebrand disconnected, he could hear a car pull up at the gate. A guard came running a few moments later. 'Comrade Firebrand. A man is at the gate claiming he is your son. There is a woman in the car he says is his mother.'

'They are, Suman. Let them in.'

XIX

Soldiers on both sides of the river, the residents of Tantilash and Calcutta and numerous towns, cities and villages were also perplexed by the sky that day. No one had ever seen such darkness in the daytime before. It was as if the Devil had spat it out of his imagination.

With Firebrand's announcement on Radio Liberation about the impending storm, the people of Sands started to move towards the concrete shelters along with their belongings and livestock. The movement of the millions continued for many hours till it began to rain at around four. Exactly after an hour, the wind began to pick up. It started on the sea. The waves that crashed into the Republican Navy and WI Navy's gigantic warships parked 250 nautical miles off the coastline were growing bigger and taller. Soon, the waves started crashing onto the decks of the supercarriers. Admiral Townsend asked the ships to get closer to each other and told the troopers to be prepared for any emergency. Then he went into the ship's hold and relieved Admiral Limpdick. The two Admirals stood on the massive deck of WIS *Matt Gusby* as the giant waves kept crashing onto it.

'This is like no storm I've ever seen, Dicky.'

'It's the birth of the new world.'

'It sure looks like the end of the one we are on right now.'

'Black Panther said none of us would be going home.'

'Are they going to kill us all?'

'Who knows.'

Nida Dodi was furious. 'If the PRC rebels can issue a cyclone warning and execute a mass evacuation, why can't you with all the technology at your disposal? I want a written clarification. Is that clear?' she barked at the Met Department Director over the phone.

'But Madame President, there were no signs of anything like this. And this isn't a cyclone, more like a gale with heavy rains.'

'Have you looked at the sky, you sisterfucker? I said: in writing. Is that difficult to understand?'

'Sorry, Madame President. I'll do the needful.'

When Laila and Ryan walked into the General's quaint cottage at 11 that morning, Firebrand was addressing the people on the radio, his back to the door. A soldier gestured at them to stay silent.

The bursts of constant shelling and machine-gun fire could be heard. Through the last half hour of their drive, the sound had only grown louder.

'This is no skirmish, Dad,' Ryan said as Firebrand got up from his chair and turned around.

'This is war. Thousands and thousands of men and women on either side, many thousands of whom will not breathe tomorrow. Just yesterday, the toll was 2,800 dead and more than 5,000 injured. Thousands of artillery pieces, tanks . . . This is no movie, son. This is about the river turning red, rotting bodies on the banks, this is about humans braving the dance of death to protect their freedom. This is about a bullet whizzing past your head, gently whispering into your ears that tomorrow you may not be so lucky.'

'I see you haven't lost even an iota of that gift of the gab,' Laila quipped.

'I'll make some tea,' Firebrand smiled, not looking at her.

'Your beard looks horrible. When was the last time you had a bath and wore a clean shirt, Roy?'

Firebrand looked at Laila, still smiling. 'Black, right?'

'Yes.'

'Lai, I took a bath two days ago and these are as fresh as they come. Can't do a thing about the mud and the dirt in the trenches.'

It had been a while since someone had called her 'Lai'. Laila liked it although she did not like the feeling of liking it at all.

Firebrand went into the kitchen and put the kettle on. He tore two pieces of bread and put them in a bowl of milk. Then he went out into the backyard and called: 'Bhombol!'

The dog that had watched over him through the night came running up. 'Bhombol has been keeping me company.'

'He looks good, Dad.'

'I try to give him something substantial or other. Not that I have much variety. But then, pariahs are easy to please.'

Firebrand picked up the intercom to the guardroom at the gate. 'Jino, who's on duty today?'

'Me, Aston, Thapa, Ananta, Suman and Dorjee, sir.'

'Could you come over with Ananta, please?'

'Right away, sir.'

Laila found the cottage rather amusing. It was quaint and colonial but spartan. The Roy she knew was used to certain comforts she had thought he could not live without.

As the two guards walked in, Firebrand took out his wallet and gave some money to Ananta. Laila recognized the tattered wallet. She had bought it from a Bata store for him five years into their marriage. 'I hear you're a great cook. Could you please get some fresh fish and mutton and cook it for us? I usually do my own thing but today I don't have time. Is that OK?'

'Yes, of course, sir, but I'm a village man. My cooking may not suit your guests' palate, General.'

'Don't worry about that. Make it like you would at home. Buy in liberal quantities, Ananta, two to three kinds of fish at least. You chaps will be eating here too. And make sure there are enough leftovers to last a few days. The next couple of days will be tricky. Do you need more money?'

'No, General, this is more than enough.' Ananta and Jino saluted Firebrand and left.

'Dad, how far is the frontline?'

'About two kilometres as the crow flies. There's a binocular set up in the room upstairs that gives you a clear view. It's got a night-vision mode as well. I have to go to the front now. You two get some rest, eat your lunch. The sheets and pillow covers are fresh. So are the towels. The bathroom's reasonably clean. I'll see you when I see you.'

Firebrand handed Ryan and Laila their coffee and then looked at his watch. It was 12.15 p.m. Eight hours to go before the spectacle would unfold.

'Dad, can I come with you?'

'Yes, but you can't stay for long. It's too risky.'

'I want to come too. I'll get bored by myself here,' said Laila.

'OK, but take your inhaler and anti-allergic medicine with you. The gunpowder smell and the slush will get to you.'

'Roy, will you ever stop behaving like my father?'

On the way, General Firebrand's vehicle stopped in front of a house. Laila and Ryan followed Firebrand inside where soldiers gave them ballistic vests and leg guards as well as helmets. Once the four-wheel drive resumed its journey, Laila and Ryan could see the wave of destruction on two sides of the mud track.

Skeletons of houses, charred vehicles, bombed-out tanks and artillery guns. As they neared the river, they could see plumes of smoke rising from here and there, and shells landing.

'Jacob, stop,' Firebrand ordered after crossing a checkpoint about 600 metres from the riverfront. 'This is where you guys get off.'

As he stepped out, Colonel Suleiman came running up to him and saluted.

'At ease, Colonel. This is my son and his mother. They wanted to see what we have been up to here. I want you to take them to Khalili Manzil. The interiors are heavily fortified and there are proper bathrooms. Set up two binoculars for them at a twin-sniper gate, no higher than the first floor. Depute some men and women to them and arrange for some drinking water.'

'Absolutely, Comrade Firebrand. This way, ma'am. Please follow me.' As Suleiman spoke, three artillery shells landed just 60 metres ahead of where they were standing.

'In you go,' shouted Firebrand as he rushed to his vehicle. Laila and Ryan, still shaking from the impact of the shells, saw the heavy vehicle bump along on the muddy road and disappear into the smokescreen created by the shells.

Khalili Manzil was without doubt the most well-constructed of the houses in the alley. It was almost 200 years old and had 24-inch-thick solid walls which only old-age masonry could have built. With two rows of gunny sacks stacked against them, they would pose a good challenge to the best of the latest tank rounds. Upon Colonel Suleiman's instructions, two bullet-proof glass plates were fastened to hooks in front of the binoculars. Ryan and Laila were handed two wireless sets. 'You can directly reach the General,' Major Hmar said. Major Bhavna trained Laila's binoculars on a dugout. 'There, ma'am. You can see General Firebrand marshal the front from his command post.'

Laila could see Firebrand manning what looked like a massive gun and shouting orders into a radio next to him. She panned a little to the side, and saw mortar shells being loaded and fired, soldiers in trenches firing their guns. She could see bodies scattered on the beach. One body did not have a head.

As Ryan and Laila sat there, soaking in all that view of death, destruction and defiance, a company of troopers passed by. The company commander sang as the soldiers joined the chorus:

'All for one and one for all,
Madame President had a great fall.
We put Adam Bum up on that wall,
He was all of five feet tall.
We screwed his ass till he was short of a ball,
His groans sounded just like a monkey's call'

Ryan burst out laughing.

'You like it?' asked Hmar.

'It's funny.'

'General Firebrand pens them from time to time.'

'Of course, who else would think of—' Laila had not finished when a rocket barrage pounded the frontline. The sound was deafening and the dugouts and machine-gun positions on the riverfront were covered in smoke and dust. Then the ambulances began rushing to the positions. Stretchers were hurried into the trenches.

Both Ryan and Laila were worried. Major Bhavna turned to her wireless set and assured them: 'The General is fine. He is holding a meeting right now.'

This was soon followed by a bombardment of the defensive lines on the other side of the river as the long-range artillery pieces that FB had positioned almost 30 kilometres from the front let go of their steam. More than 50 guns fired about 10 rounds each as soldiers perched on rooftops and minarets in Devil's Lair guided them to the positions to be shelled.

Ryan turned to Bhavna. 'So what made you join this war?'

'I was an engineering student when they disbanded the workers and students unions and started putting opposition politicians in jails. My father was a dockyard workers-union organizer. The secret police came home one night. They picked him up. He was found three days later, dead in a ditch. His bones were broken, his nails had been pulled out. A few days later, a friend from college introduced me to a PRC sympathizer. And there was no looking back.'

'I am so sorry,' Laila said.

'Don't be—because I'm not. I was posted to Major Aks' unit which was a part of General Firebrand's brigade. He was a

Colonel then but he commanded much bigger forces. Since I had an engineering background, I took to communications like a fish to water. I was part of the first battalion when we took Calcutta. My mother and younger brother were in the crowd waving flags at us as our trucks rolled in. They looked so proud. It was such an emotional moment. There were banners everywhere. A grand concert was held at the Maidan where musicians performed and poets read out from their works. Colonel Firebrand's message was read out by El Comandante.'

'El Comandante is Uncle Longbeard,' Ryan explained to his mother.

'Why was his message read out? Where was he? I mean your Firebrand,' asked Laila.

'He was shot in the leg. He was in hospital. I went to visit him once with some lamb my mother had cooked. He ate it with such relish.'

'Oh, give him anything that once walked on four legs and he's the happiest.'

Colonel Suleiman walked up the stairs, his heavy boots thumping against the wooden stairs.

'Ma'am, sir. Comrade Firebrand is here. Please come down.'

XX

Firebrand, Laila and Ryan had an early dinner that evening. In fact, the whole of Sands did as they had been advised over the radio in repeat broadcasts of General Firebrand's address. Food packets were distributed in the shelters. Generators were plugged in at hospitals. The power plants and mines were shut, the factories closed, the blast furnaces in the steel plants switched off. Cars, buses and trucks stayed off the roads. People who had brick-and-cement homes stayed indoors.

Then came the thunderstorm at 7 p.m. sharp. On Firebrand's instructions, the PRC Guerrillas had folded up their tents and moved into the houses and buildings of Devil's Lair by 5. The heavy weaponry was carted out, leaving behind some mortars, machine guns and rifles to respond to firing from across the river. But the Republican forces had no warning. There were no major settlements on the other bank, so they jostled for space in the dugouts which could hold only a few hundred. The remaining thousands saw their tents blown to tatters and their supplies become wet and soggy. They themselves were drenched to the bone.

The intense storm lasted for just half an hour following which Firebrand drove down to the frontline with Laila and Ryan.

'Roy, I'm dead tired, I've told you a hundred times already. This better be something exceptional.'

'Trust me, Lai, you don't want to miss this.'

The vehicle drove with its headlights turned off so as to not be an easy target for enemy gunfire. Laila and Ryan could tell that it veered left from where they had been headed earlier in the day. 'Are we going to a different part of town, Dad?'

'Yes, to the best vantage point that Devil's Lair has to offer.'

The vehicle screeched to a halt on a vacant field with patchy grass and two bamboo football goalposts at its two ends. A giant watchtower stood at a distance, the same one on which the long-horned bird had breathed its last. Colonel Aks and Major Bhavna were waiting for them at the foot of the long winding stairs. They climbed up first, followed by Laila, Ryan and Firebrand. There were two sentries at the top.

Once they got there, they sat down on chairs with straps attached. Firebrand asked everyone to buckle up. 'I have some dry fruits and nuts and a few bottles of water in this bag. Ryan, keep this with you.'

From the watchtower, the entire town of Devil's Lair was visible below them. They could see the silhouettes of the remains of the bombed-out buildings whose tops seemed to merge with the blackness of the sky. The twin white culverts of the broken bridge that connected the two banks even a year ago stood out like an old man's gaping maw. The troops on the other side were visible too, though not very clearly, more like a dark patch.

It was 8 p.m. in Sands when at the Hollow up on the Bald Mountain, Aurelio and Sitaram returned from the well, drenched, and sat down in front of the large earthen frying pan. Once Olga lit the earthen lamps on either side, the geometric patterns she had drawn around it with turmeric and chilli powder became clearly visible. The thread was dug well into the clay model of the landmass, down to the very bottom.

Sitaram folded his hands and began chanting, 'O Creator and Destroyer of the Universe, heed us. O Arbiter of Life and Death, listen to us.'

His voice grew louder and louder. Blind Hyena and Sloth Bear sat quietly behind Olga.

'It's on your command that the Sun rises, it's on your instruction that rain falls on Earth, it's by your wish that the wind blows.'

Olga had laid some traps in the jungle the day before and managed to catch three jungle fowls. She had brought them in and tied them in the corner to a rock slab. Now they began making strange noises. The cave was loaded with firewood which Elan's men had brought in the morning with rice, grams, potato, oil and vegetables. There was enough food to last a few weeks.

'So, accept this humble drink, O Lord Almighty, served by this lady. Have you partaken of the soma?'

Olga poured the alcohol from the pitcher in her hand onto the little mound of earth on top of the clay model, the same one on which Sitaram had drawn two eyes, a nose and a mouth a few days ago.

Sitaram's voice reached a frenzied pitch. 'This wine gives you strength that you may pass on to us. For your strength is our strength. Your deed is our deed. Without you, we are nothing. And we need all your strength, O Lord. So, have you partaken of the soma?'

Olga poured some more alcohol on the mound.

'Bless us Lord for we are only acting on your behalf. It is you who made this world. And it is you who will unmake the same. It is in your name and by your wish that we start the making of a new world here on the Island of Bald Mountain. So, have you partaken of the soma?'

Olga poured the rest of the alcohol as Sitaram grabbed the two ends of the thread sticking out of the clay model and pulled vigorously. Soon, a part of the clay model broke off with a cracking sound and crashed into the southern side of the earthen pan.

The seven people seated on the top of the watchtower facing the northwest felt a strong jerk as the entire landmass to the east of the Ganges broke off from the Indian plate and started drifting south. The waters of the river began to swell as the landmass set off towards the sea. The expanse of water grew bigger and bigger till the other side was no longer in sight.

Waves crashed into the pier. Laila and Ryan were spellbound for the first 10 to 15 minutes but soon their faces bore the unmistakable mark of acute fear. They were drifting into the ocean, into the darkness, into the unknown.

The entire population of Sands and the Republic felt the tremor for a few seconds. The fisherfolk and the few PRC units towards the south of Sands, where the mangrove forests adorned the delta islands along the creeks and estuaries that opened into the sea, felt they were riding a giant ship into the ocean. The movement was palpable yet smooth. Save for the initial jerk, there were no aftershocks. In the north, the Himalayas stood tall and firm in their wait for an address again. Those who dwelled in the cities, towns and villages inland felt very little movement but those near the digging lines felt like castaways sailing into the endless waters.

The sonar on the ships of the Joint Naval Task Force had been beeping nonstop. As Admiral Limpdick, Admiral Townsend, Vice-Admiral Choksi and the senior crew on board WIS *Enterprise* stared with horror at the satellite feeds that showed the giant landmass gliding towards their fleet at a breathtaking 60 knots per hour, the radio silence in the mission control room was broken by a hello.

'Yes, Admiral Townsend here.'

'Evening, Admiral, this is Marshal Ivan Bagramyan, born 1897, died 1982. As should be amply clear to you, the ships and submarines of your fleet cannot escape collision. You are not even 150 nautical miles away as we speak. I am going to give you some coordinates. You have to ask all your subs to surface and steer them and your ships into the pathways. That will move them into the estuaries and creeks and prevent a direct collision with the continental slope. Since the movement of the landmass is going to create a cyclical movement of waters in these gaps, you can switch off your engines and simply use the mechanical brakes to stay clear of the shore and each other. Are you following me, Admiral?'

'Yes, Marshal.'

'Please note down the coordinates. I am not going to repeat them.'

It was early morning in the eastern parts of the World Island when Adam Bum found himself seated at the command centre in the Trapezium, the headquarters of the WI Department of Defence, along with his top commanders and noted sycophants. As he chewed on a stale turkey sandwich, in front of him, on the giant screen, a 500,000-square-kilometre landmass was darting towards his fleet of over 60 of the world's most state-of-the-art warships.

The independent country of Sands, along with its contiguous Seven Hills province, was swimming its way to the Island of Bald Mountain.

XXI

Exactly 29 hours later, in the wee hours of the morning according to the new time zone into which the landmass had drifted, the castaway Republic of Sands docked at the southern continental slope of the Island of Bald Mountain. Sailing past the island with the massive brown peak on its left, it had floated leftward before locking itself into position. The forbidding Himalayan heights towards the north of Sands stood at a distance of 30 kilometres from the beaches that flanked the tropical jungles in the south. The two islands were now a 90-minute ferry ride away from each other.

After spending a few hours at the watchtower, Firebrand, Laila and Ryan had returned to the cottage. For the first time in four years, not a single bullet was fired at night. No air-raid sirens rang out. The people of Sands slept soundly. So did Roy, Laila and Ryan.

The next morning, the power plants kicked back into action. The factories too, though mining operations remained on hold. Fishermen were cautioned to keep close to shore, and river ferries stayed anchored to their floats by the jetties. Slowly, some shops opened for business. Life on Sands began to return to normal.

Firebrand set off towards Calcutta for an emergency meeting of the PRC Military Council. Laila and Ryan said they would go as well. Before they set out, he had a long conversation with Kapo; they decided that the five top commanders would meet before the larger session.

'You should go on radio, Kapo. People need to know.'

'I will. FB, what do you think happens now? Even a part of the Seven Hills province has broken away.'

'As a separate piece?'

'Nope. We're like conjoined twins floating in the sea.'

'How big?'

'Don't know, FB. But reports are coming in that it could be all of it.'

'Don't worry. It can only make things better. Without Sands and the Seven Hills, the Republic is a lame horse. We can ask the Seven Hills to join us. Or they can do their own thing. We have no beef with them. We'll survive, Kapo. We may have to struggle but we will survive.'

'I hope so, FB.'

In the car, Firebrand, Laila, Ryan and Jacob listened to El Comandante's address to the nation. He explained to the people what had happened and asked them not to panic. He also said Sands had enough fuel and foodstock to last well over two years and that a part of the mineral-rich Seven Hills province had also broken off and was now floating away alongside Sands. 'Our aspirations of nationhood and a better society have been answered by Mother Nature. Now, the road ahead is one of cohesion, hard work and peace. Look at the sky. The darkness is fading away. A new era dawns. It is up to us to embrace it and build a brand-new world.'

There was absolute silence in the Tantilash war room when Madame President walked in. The senior cabinet members were already in place. You had to be really senior to be a senior minister in Nida Dodi's cabinet—they were all men and women well into their 70s who held no power, only portfolios. Take the Minister of Transport and Higher Education: he was more famous for castigating the students of Tantilash Central University for the used condoms and liquor bottles that his team had reportedly collected before one of his visits to the institution. One day, his secretary brought him some documents requiring his signature: Madame President had decided to withdraw all state support to higher education and sell the universities to private operators. He had no clue about any of it. He signed the papers. He had no choice. Nida Dodi's was a one-woman cabinet. There was only one window for clearance, only one decision-maker.

But even Nida Dodi, who had never tendered an apology for any action or decision, was deep in thought that morning as the presidential limousine drove her to her office. She had learnt about the Seven Hills province breaking off with Sands. She clearly remembered that afternoon five years ago when she had stepped onto a stage somewhere in a Calcutta suburb. A stage built at one end of a huge field; journalists had estimated that there were over 150,000 in attendance. In the course of her speech, she had declared that the entire province of Sands was to be turned into a Special Economic Zone: it would become the factory of the world. Hence, it had to be replanned and reshaped, and some people would have to surrender their land for that grand scheme to be launched. New townships would come up, new ports would be set up, and so on and so forth. Murmurs of protest had begun to ripple through the crowd almost instantly. And soon they grew louder and louder, until her voice was drowned by the shouting. Nida Dodi had carried on, undaunted: 'This is my decision. It's up to you to vacate the land voluntarily, or wait for me to force you off. The SEZ will be built, no matter what.'

When Tantilash nudged the governor of Sands, the provincial authorities notified the districts about the timeline for land acquisition. When the district authorities tried to take possession, they were met with fierce resistance from the people. The police was deployed, but since nearly all of them hailed from Sands and stood to lose their own land, they defected to the peoples' protest. Then the central paramilitary and military forces were brought in; the peoples' army retaliated with their muskets and one-shot country-made guns. Sadly, many were killed and many more jailed. Soon, the resistance fighters fled into the inaccessible jungles and the mountainous region to the north; there they organized and armed themselves, held camps for military training and chalked out plans for assaults. In less than two years, the resistance morphed into the PRC Guerrillas, a half-a-million-strong fighting unit, equipped with modern weapons and skills.

First, they took the towns and villages near the foothills and armed and organized the locals. The Republican collaborators were summarily executed. In less than a year, the Republican forces were completely pushed out. Calcutta fell, so did the other towns in the Gangetic plains. The resistance peaked after defections from the armed forces. It was a curious mix: Marxist–Leninists, Marxist–Maoists, regional nationalists, remnants of the old Justice Party, former armed forces and police personnel, the clergy of nearly every faith, agnostics, farmers, workers, the petty bourgeois. Usually they would be at each other's throats, but the prospect of being uprooted brought them together.

Nida Dodi had planned a 200-foot-tall gateway built out of the heads of the resistance fighters in Calcutta—she wanted to ride into the city through it. She wanted to drag down all the resistance leaders to Tantilash, and have them lynched on the floor of the National Stadium. She wanted to raze Calcutta to the ground, and then rebuild it to her liking. She wanted to chain the people to the factories and ports she would build there. The revenge on Sands had to be so exemplary that no one would ever dream of seceding from the Republic again.

But for now, her plans had to be put on hold. The sea stood between the wishes of Madame President and their realization. This would take more preparation, more time, more effort, a logistical overhaul. The mineral and oil-rich Seven Hills and coal-rich Sands were gone for the time being. As Madame President alighted from her car, Sands and the Seven Hills were still on the move.

The meeting ended with Madame President making her decision clear to the cabinet: Sands and the Seven Hills were still very much inalienable and integral parts of the Republic. But the navy's expeditionary capabilities had to be expanded to extend Tantilash's writ on those lands. She wanted it done within a year. 'If they think by floating away, they can escape the justice of Nida Dodi and subvert the territorial integrity of the Republic, they are fools.'

XXII

The Island of Bald Mountain had been almost 2,900 kilometres from Sands two weeks ago. Now it was a mere 30 kilometres away. On the other hand, the distance between the Republic and the island had grown to 3,450 kilometres. From the southern tip of Sands, Oceania was a little over 2,000 kilometres away. The United Nations had never faced such a situation in its history.

Following the docking of the landmass, the Republican authorities and armed forces in the Seven Hills surrendered themselves to the PRC Guerrillas under pressure from the locals who had no bones to grind with Sands and had always felt hard done by the mainland Republic. While Tantilash and Davnagar flourished on the mineral and oil riches of the Seven Hills, the province got little in return. Since they were mainly tribal societies, the mainland Republic had always treated them with disdain.

A meeting was organized between the PRC top brass and the tribal chiefs of the Seven Hills province, who approved of the deal that PRC offered them: either a unified country or a land of their own. They readily chose the latter. If it worked, they said, would all mull a union.

'But we should have a mutual non-aggression pact,' said El Comandante.

'Absolutely, and I think we must come to each other's help in war and peace even if we are separate nations,' replied Biaksiama, leader of the biggest tribe. All the other elders agreed.

'Open borders, visa-free travel, right to work, study, settle, stay with dignity. We should be civilized. Our children should grow up in a land without hatred. But if someone brings hate to our doorstep, they should be given a fitting answer,' said Firebrand. The Seven Hills leaders clapped in agreement.

The missives seeking recognition as new countries reached the United Nations from Sands and the Seven Hills at about the same time that World Island Navy's Pacific fleet was closing in on the Island of Bald Mountain from the east. President Bum had asked for the return of the Task Force fleet, the warplanes, the captured pilots and the sailors. The PRC had replied that an exchange of prisoners would only happen via mediation by a body like the UN. Though they were ready to release the spy.

The United Nations went into a total tizzy. While the World Island supported the Republic's contention that the two territories be treated as a part of the latter, the Eurasians opposed it. Some of the European partners in the Coalition of the Righteous voiced their opinion in support of the new territories. According to them, treating the territories as belonging to the

Republic, despite the wishes of the people, reeked of colonialism. It's another matter that just a month ago, the same lot had unanimously voted against a clause mooted by Mali and Central African Republic condemning the European colonists for atrocities and economic exploitation. What if Asia, Africa and South America asked for reparations from the European nations for hundreds of years of colonial exploitation, and they had to comply? The European powers had shuddered at the prospect of this eventuality in the closed-door meeting before the vote.

Finally, it was decided that PRC and the Seven Hills should also have their say on the floor of the United Nations in the City of No Sleep. The Republic and World Island grudgingly accepted the suggestion, though World Island had a condition: the UN would have to ensure that its defence personnel in PRC captivity were alive and well, and somehow make possible the process of bringing them back. The UN agreed. In their turn, the PRC rebels and the Seven Hills tribal chiefs asked for a guarantee of no harm and diplomatic immunity for its delegates, as the City of No Sleep was located in mainland World Island. The UN Secretary General promptly responded that it was not a problem at all.

President Bum was livid about the whole thing, but his advisors convinced him of the need for the World Island to behave like a peaceful, responsible member of the UN. 'In the game of global perception, at times you have to play like a cat and extend a warm, soft paw and keep the sharp claws hidden. Our Navy is closing in. Let them shout all they want. If it comes to separate nationhood, we will veto it and put our forces to action,' said Frank.

Nida Dodi also weighed the pros and cons of waging war in order to reclaim a territory that now lay thousands of kilometres away. Of course, the idea of the SEZ was now dead. But Sands still had coal, oil, limestone, quartzite, manganese; the Seven Hills a lot of oil and all the uranium, bauxite, copper and iron ore you could imagine. It would be much more expensive to transport it all back to the Republic, but that was nothing compared with the retributive urge that was pounding in her brain. Even if Sands and the Seven Hills were nothing but barren desert, Madame President would bring the people to justice, albeit her brand of it.

Sands had been limping back to a semblance of normality after undergoing the change of coordinates. The Seven Hills took a little longer, for it had not prepared for such an eventuality. But Sands and the PRC administration extended every possible kind of help. A few countries here and there began to send their envoys, and corporations sent their representatives to enquire about the prospects of buying coal, oil and minerals. Some even began to do business with them. Banks were set up with guidance from economists.

It was at one such business meeting with a Petro Oceania delegation that an impish thought occurred to Biaksiama. At the end of the meeting, he dialled El Comandante, who heard him about and then said: 'I'll talk to the others. I think they'll agree. Let's go for it. Hope they take the bait.'

The next evening, at a dinner hosted at Biaksiama's house, the members of the Petro Oceania delegation were getting high on chhang, sipping at their wooden straws stuck into bamboo barrels into which boiling water had been poured over semi-fermented millet seeds.

Biaksiama waited for the right moment, and then took one of them out for a smoke.

Less than 72 hours later, the government of Oceania staked its claim to Sands and the Seven Hills, saying that the southern tip of the landmass lay just 220 kilometres north of its territory, Spinster Island.

The UN had always been a circus. This was the moment that it became circus maximus.

No one, of course, paid any attention to the tiny island that lay 30 kilometres north of Sands. At 3,400 square kilometres, it was far too small to be worth anyone's while. It was not possible for anyone to know that this entire tectonic shift, and the realignment of nation states, had been orchestrated from a crater in an island inhabited by a tribal community that had never come in contact with the outside world before Aurelio, Sitaram and Olga's rickety boat arrived on their shores a little over two and a half years ago.

More often than not, we ignore the little things, dismiss them as insignificant. If you would have met General Firebrand, and in the rare eventuality that he opened up to you, he would have told you the same. The warning signs had come when he started relying on alcohol to forget things. Roy had been abusing alcohol for a long time, but it became more pronounced after they moved to Davnagar when Ryan had been about three years old. The list of things he wanted to forget grew with time. And the drinking wasn't entirely in vain. He did start forgetting: phone numbers, what he had been doing the night before, passages from books he'd known like the back of his hand, his e-mail and phone passwords. What he really wanted to forget were Laila's mood swings, his father dying like a pig in a hospital bed, his hands and legs tied to the posts as he writhed in pain. Then his mother's death while he was travelling. The non-receipt of his salary, the oppressive boredom at his work-place, the mediocrity everywhere he turned, the rise of the fascist Republic, the passive apartment dwellers and their robotic lives. But these he remembered over and over again. He withdrew into a shell, cut himself off from his friends. Most of his good friends had in any case moved back to Calcutta, a city Laila hated and would never contemplate going back to.

The more depressed he got, the more he drank. And the more he drank, the deeper the depression grew. On some nights, he would wash down two litres of whisky with packs and packs of cigarettes. A distance developed between him and Lai. Then one night, everything exploded between them. They went to a marriage counsellor, and he said it was possibly a one-off inci-dent, that they could no doubt work it all out. But after a few weeks, they collided again. This time, Roy stopped drinking for a few months, and Lai began to believe he was finally chang-ing for the better. But just as they had rediscovered their old romance, and he began to have an occasional drink or two—he lost it again. This third time he lost Lai and Ryan too, for good. The worst thing of all was that he had no memory of what he had done. Alcohol had rewired his brain to such an extent that when he drank, he was no longer forgetting—no memory was simply being formed.

It is a cardinal sin to cast away the little things as insignificant, to treat poor people as expendable, to ignore the small signs. General Firebrand had learnt it the hard way.

But President Bum and Madame President had not. Not yet.

XXIII

'It's a mindfuck,' exclaimed Aurelio, lifting his eyes from the pitcher from which he had been pouring date wine into the small earthen bowls around which Sitaram, Olga, Begum Johnson and Civet Cat sat huddled. Raven, perched on a hunk of rock, said: 'Saucers at play.' Then he flapped his wings and flew down and sat beside the other five.

Just a day earlier, the UN delegation had flown down to Sands and met the captured World Island sailors, airmen and frogmen in the presence of the international press. Flanked by Admiral Limpdick, Vice-Admiral Varun Choksi and other senior officers, Admiral Townsend said to the TV cameras: 'All the soldiers in the Joint Task Force have had an awakening. We realize the misery and cruelty we have inflicted on extensive parts of the world in the name of defending our homeland. What we have done is immoral and unethical. Only the corporations and the billionaires have profited from the blood of our fellowmen. We stand by Sands and the Seven Hills who are trying to defend their freedom from those who want to subjugate them and steal their resources. Freedom is their natural right, and we will stand and fight with them. Our eyes have opened, and they will not close again. We will never be on the wrong side again. We call upon our brothers and sisters in the World Island Navy and Republican Navy to join us on the right side. We appeal to our respective citizens to see the light.'

The news spread like wildfire. There was a mutiny on board the ships of the Joint Task Force of the World Island Navy and the Republican Navy. Even the officers joined in.

A few hours later, Admiral Simon Connoway, Commander of the World Island Navy's Pacific Fleet, got a radio message from WIS *Enterprise*. It was Admiral Limpdick, his senior at the naval college and mentor: 'Your ships are 400 nautical miles from the Seven Hills. Turn around immediately or we will engage.'

Admiral Connoway contacted the Trapezium at once. His fleet was around 20-strong and had two supercarriers. The enemy had nearly 60 warships including 5 supercarriers and one regular carrier. He was ordered to retreat by 200 nautical miles and await instructions.

A quick meeting of the UNSC was convened, and the council appealed for an immediate emergency session of the member nations in the presence of representatives from Sands and the Seven Hills.

The next day, a special UN aircraft landed in Calcutta only to depart that same night. Colonel Aks, Brigadier General Paddy and Brigadier Maria were handpicked to represent Sands. Kapo came to the tarmac. So did Firebrand. He shook hands with all three at the foot of the stairs.

A car arrived and Laila and Ryan stepped out of it with their luggage. Firebrand saw the big olive-green bag he had given Ryan. He hugged Ryan, 'You stay good, son, and out of trouble.'

'You too, Dad.'

'You've grown up to be a fine, strong man. Just don't make the mistakes I did. Goodbye, Ryan.'

Then Roy turned to Laila with a smile. 'Let me take your bag.'

He took the bag and walked up the stairs and into the plane. 'Still a light traveller, huh?'

'Yes, as always.'

Ryan and Laila followed him up. After he put the bag in the overhead bin, Roy instinctively reached out his hand to pat Laila on the cheek but checked himself. 'You take care, Lai.'

'You be careful, too, Roy. Stop smoking.'

'I better get off now.'

'Roy,' Laila called out. He turned.

'It was good to see you. Take good care of yourself.'

Roy nodded with a smile. Deep inside, he felt wobbly. His world was slipping away yet again. He was desperately seeking the soldier in him to come to the rescue. Roy needed to become General Firebrand again. But as he stood on the tarmac and saw the aircraft roar away towards the City of No Sleep, he did not feel like a soldier.

Fate can be a merciless sculptor. It can pick cruelty as its chosen chisel. It can carve away the softer parts to begin with, leaving a little bit here and there to work on many years later. In-between, it turns its hand to carving the harder matter. What it intends to create, we do not know.

XXIV

The sudden change of heart by the personnel of the Joint Task Force was obviously a huge surprise even to the PRC command. Firebrand advised Kapo to be wary.

'This could be a ploy.'

'I'm with you there, FB.'

'By the way, I'm very proud of Aks. He was so forceful and eloquent. I think our case is extremely strong, and it'll be difficult even for that Bum bastard to veto it.'

'He's your boy, FB. I knew he was special from the way you spoke of him. He certainly left a huge impression. Every paper, every TV station was full of praise for his clarity of thought and expression. I guess the fact that he's a handsome lad adds to it. He was trending on the internet, I checked.'

'I think Maria spoke very well too, about the provisional government's vision to integrate Sands with the world. And Paddy, my God! How does he know so much about renewable energy and sustainable agriculture, Kapo?'

'Oh, he's always reading, FB. Something you and I used to do.'

'I think it would be good to appoint him Minister of Agriculture and Energy when we draw up the list. When do you think we'll go public with that?'

'As soon as they're back, FB. By the way, what role do you see for yourself in this new scheme of things? Defence, culture? Maybe both.'

'Nah! I'm not cut out for any of this shit. These days I get tired way too soon. I want to retire to the mountains, play my ukulele. Write a bit. Grow some vegetables. Some flowers. I've always wanted to. Though I know I need to do something to put the food on my plate. I have to figure that out.'

'You should quit smoking. You're getting out of breath even after a minute's walk. And I've noticed you clutching your chest from time to time. Go for a check-up, FB. I think the mountains are a good idea. The air will be good for you.'

'I will.'

'Quit cigarettes, or see a doc?'

'The latter, Kapo. At my age, it's difficult to kick bad habits.'

'You're not that much older than me, FB. Come on.'

'Age is mind and experience over matter and theory, Kapo. There, I am no less than a 200-year-old Buddhist monk. And you are a 50-something John Hancock.'

'In that case, we should embalm you,' Kapo grinned.

'Yes, if you can afford it. They're spending close to 300,000 dollars a year to preserve Lenin.'

'That much? I wonder if they would have done it had they known.'

'They probably would have. Stalin took charge of the funeral. You think he'd have flinched one bit?'

'I'm not so sure.'

'Did you know that Krupskaya had wanted Lenin buried? And that it took the Soviets 56 days to decide on the embalmment?'

'That long? But wouldn't the body be hellrotten by then?'

'Russian winter, Kapo. The best freezer known to man.'

'Good to see your memory coming back.'

'Only in fits and starts.'

'Better than what it used to be, right?'

'Maybe.'

'FB, can I ask you something personal?'

'Depends on how personal.'

'How was it? Seeing them after this long?'

'That's too personal.'

'There used to be a time when you'd share everything with me.'

'There used to be a time when I had a family to call my own. I had a name. Things have changed.'

The click of a lighter had both El Comandante and Firebrand turn towards the right.

Black Panther lit a cigar and took two deep puffs. 'Sorry to butt in. Not that you guys were discussing anything important.'

'How did you get in, spooky cat,' said El Comandante as he looked towards the wooden swinging door.

'There is a reason why we jaguars are called the stealthiest predators of the forest,' Black Panther bared his fangs in glee. 'Could you pass me the ashtray, General?'

'You came through the window. You have a thing for them,' said Firebrand as he pushed the ashtray across the table.

'Absolutely. The fun of sneaking up on someone is unparalleled. Didn't you do that as a child? Hide behind doors and pounce on unsuspecting others? The only difference is that since we do this for survival, we are way better at it than you. Now, listen carefully. There is a place, a small island, 30 kilometres to the north of Sands. It's got some lovely beaches and a lagoon of green waters. No one from Sands or the Seven Hills must set foot there. No travellers, no explorers, no boats.'

'OK. I don't think anyone even knows about it,' said Kapo.

'Yet it needs protection. Bum and Dodi would like to use it as a launch pad for operations against you. That can't happen. That's neither good news for you, nor for the inhabitants of that island.'

'How many people on it? Which country?' said Firebrand.

'About 30,000 endogamous tribals in the forest villages. They've never met an outsider, hence they've been spared the poisonous fruits of the Industrial Revolution and its descendants.

No country. There are a few such islands all over the Indian Ocean archipelagos.'

'And how do we defend it without setting foot on it?' said Kapo.

'You station a small part of your Navy to its northwest and southeast. That will work as a deterrent. It's a strong force. Setting foot on the island is your last option. And that too, only soldiers.'

'Look, we don't know if these Navy guys are pulling a fast one on us. What if—'

Firebrand was cut short by the beast's growl.

'You know, FB, you have to start trusting people again. Your fears are totally unfounded. They are firmly on your side.'

'Magic again?'

'A combination of magic and science.'

Black Panther did not give any more details. Nor did Firebrand and Kapo ask for any. But you, the reader of these pages, are a different creature. Your curiosity knows no limits.

Do you remember when Marshal Bhodi had opened the Chamber of Saucers? Some of the saucers had been razor-thin discs invisible to the naked eye. Now, there happens to be a psychosurgical procedure called leucotomy where most connections to and from the prefrontal cortex are scraped away. The surgery was controversial and was scrapped sometime in the last century for it was believed the same could be used to control thought and restrain individual rights.

There is another psychosurgical technique called anterior cingulotomy which can increase or decrease your emotional response to situations.

Now, a combination of the two . . . You can figure it out, right?

After Black Panther left, Firebrand got up. Kapo said, 'FB, You called me John Hancock. Who's that?'

'A fabulously wealthy man with a very stylish signature on an extremely important piece of paper. But long dead and forgotten,' Firebrand said as he left.

The twin panels of the wooden door swung to and fro for quite some time before sighing to a rest.

XXV

Dr Aaron Nahoum and Dr Avi Chaudhuri had their weekly breakfast meeting at the Police Tent on the Maidan in Calcutta that Friday morning. They had been friends from their first day in college about 30 years ago. Apart from their interest in physics, they had bonded over football. Every Friday, after classes, they would dump their bags in their Eden Hostel rooms and go off to watch the local third- and fourth-division clubs play on the vast greens of the Maidan. Saturdays and Sundays were reserved for the first-division biggies of the Calcutta Football League who could afford retired Nigerian World Cuppers and third-division players from Brazil and England.

They would sit in a distant corner of the field, chomping on peanuts, and watch the game. The matches were brutal, and referees frequently ran away to save their lives. There were fans with switch-blade knives concealed in their butter-jean trousers. At times, the blades would end up in the bellies of rival fans. Then there would be police vans and mounted cops chasing the hooligans away. After the match, they would walk back to their hostel, passing the horse-drawn carriages that gave rides to the tourists who flocked to see the Victoria Memorial. The fairy on top of the dome would rotate on its base. It no longer turns today. The last of the technicians who knew how to fix it a wee bit died a decade ago. A lot of those referees and footballers were also long gone, claimed by the electric furnaces in crematoriums or buried in the city's many cemeteries. A few had been left on the Tower of Silence in Beleghata for the crows and vultures to feast upon. Now there were hardly any Parsis left in the city. Or any vultures.

They would always stop at the Police Tent for the delectable chicken stew served with hand-made Park Circus Bakery bread, lightly toasted. That taste remained the same. When they went to pursue their PhD programmes, Aaron on nuclear physics at Cambridge and Avi on particle physics at Max Planck in Munich, they would often speak on the phone. And always talk about the chicken stew.

By the time they came back after their post-doctoral stints and joined the Saha Institute of Nuclear Physics eight years ago, Calcutta had changed. The local football clubs were mostly gone. Everyone was watching cricket or the Mega Football League where the clubs dealt in billions. The small clubs had been kicked out of their Maidan addresses which was now used by the Army and the security forces for training and exercises. The Police Tent canteen was still there. But the Police football team was nowhere to be found.

They made it a point to meet there every Friday morning, have breakfast and go to work. But ever since the Guerrillas took over Sands, they had been drawn into the resistance movement. Apart from monitoring the running of the science clubs that had been set up to promote the spread of scientific temper among the people, the duo had been entrusted with a new responsibility over the last few weeks. Which is why, every Friday morning, a military vehicle would arrive at the Police Tent canteen at 9.30 a.m. They would be blindfolded and taken to an undisclosed location where they would check on something and sign a paper, certifying that all was well.

That Friday morning too, a vehicle came and stopped in front of the Police Tent at half past nine. After a little more than 30 minutes, the vehicle came to a stop and the blindfolded duo was led into a building with a wooden staircase, the planks of which creaked in protest under their feet. Their blindfolds were removed. A squarish steel suitcase lay in front of them. An officer handed over two keys to one of the escort guards, who put them in their slots and stepped back.

Avi turned the keys, and opened the suitcase.

It was empty.

The officers immediately called up their superiors. Two minutes later, El Comandante came to know: the Lunch Box bomb was gone.

After the Sands and the Seven Hills presentations at the UN, the Republic, the WI and Oceania put forth their views. Oceania's sudden entry complicated matters for the WI and the Republic. Oceania was an old and important member of the WI-led Coalition of the Righteous. Already, the European partners in the military coalition had distanced themselves from the WI and the Republic on this issue.

Both Adam Bum and Nida Dodi had utmost disregard for the Europeans' penchant for using their rhetoric on human rights and freedom of choice as and when it suited them. Nida told Bum, 'They use compunction on a case-to-case basis. Either they are indecisive or they are crafty. Both are signs of weakness. You can't depend on such people.'

Bum had to skirt around rights issues from time to time back home, owing to pressure from the media. He called them 'a bunch of pathological liars, the main hurdles to my plans of making the WI great again.' The media in the WI was not in his full control yet. Bum admired Nida Dodi for that, for turning the watchdog and fourth pillar in the Republic into a pliable, justifying force for her policies and decisions even if that spelt doom for the people. A section of the WI media called Bum a 'racist and misogynist bigot', but this was one brown woman he actually admired.

And, of course, there were the Eurasians, the bloody Eurasians, buoyed by the rising prices of oil and gas. Most crucially, they held veto power in the security council. They had considerable military strength too, with sophisticated toys and a long history of fighting the bloodiest of wars and ending them on their terms.

Still, the most powerful country in the world could not afford to let Sands and the Seven Hills run away with nationhood and give the WI a bloody nose. But his options were more limited now, with the captured Joint Task Force sailors and airmen revolting and pledging their allegiance to Sands. They had even repainted the names of the ships. The WIS *Enterprise* was now the SNS *Awakening*. A few TV channels broadcast these images and quite a few newspapers ran editorials, panning Bum and his policies for an unprecedented revolt in the ranks and file of the military.

There was more bad news for Bum. Frank said that, in the event of a war, the Task Force fleet would run out of ammunition and supplies in less than a month. Shane informed him about the consignments of precision munition, bombs and air-to-air, air-to-ground, air-to-ship, ship-to-ship, long-range and short-range cruise missiles that had gone missing from various warehouses of the country. Huge inventories of spares and parts for aircraft and ships also could not be traced. Bum had no doubt as to where they had gone.

Bum was getting more insecure with every passing day. His re-election bid was clearly being hampered by current events. He was sitting with Frank one evening in his office and sipping some bourbon, 'It's definitely paranormal stuff. How do we win this, Frank?'

'I'm thinking, Bummer. We'll find a way.'

Bum's phone rang. It was Liz. 'Mr President, our sources tell us that the Lunch Box has been stolen. The PRC command is in a tizzy.'

'You've pulled it off, Liz. I love you.'

'It's not us, Mr President. I'll let you know when I get more news.' Liz hung up.

Bum gulped down the rest of his drink and turned towards Frank. 'Give me a cigarette, Frank.'

'Bummer?'

'Don't say anything. I need a quiet smoke. You can go now.'

Frank left. Bum got up and stood by the window that opened onto the huge lawns where his chopper was standing. As he puffed on the cigarette, he muttered: 'You think you'll take me down, you little bastard? Where are you, you shit? Who do you think you're fucking with, you little bastard . . .'

His voice grew louder and louder.

'The President is going crazy,' said the guard on the ground floor to the housekeeping maid who was walking down the corridor.

'He always was,' said the maid as she went inside and shut the door behind her.

XXVI

Firebrand was sitting on the front steps of his ground-floor flat in the once-posh Golf Green neighbourhood of Calcutta and watching the snails, the ants, the earthworms and the beetles crawling about what had once been a sprawling garden with flowering plants, papaya and lemon trees. Many, many years ago, his old man had sat on the same steps and contemplated a death that had been closing in by the hour. Now, there were no trees—only a few forlorn strands of grass struggling up here and there. But the wet earth still smelt the same, its perfume as refreshing, as raw, as unadulterated as when he'd been a 10-year-old. In fact, after years of inhaling gunpowder smell and pit-fire smoke, it smelt more heavenly than before.

When he'd walked in a few days ago, into the only place in the world he could call home, weeds and grass as tall as a man had turned the garden into a jungle dense enough for Black Panther to hide in. Creepers had staked their claim to the length, breadth and height of the balconies.

His driver Jacob called Colonel Aks and told him that the General had gone mad.

'It'll take two days for a whole army to clean up this place. I'm not even talking about the inside. And he's trying to do it himself. He's wielding the machete like Don Quixote, and clutching his chest in pain from time to time. I can see snakes slithering away through the gaps in the broken fencing.'

Aks promptly arrived with 10 of his men.

FB had dismissed Aks' suggestion that his men carry out the cleaning operation but he relented as Aks walked up to him and took the shears out of his hands. 'I lost my parents pretty early,' Aks said, 'and you're the only person I've looked up to since then. I can't let you go. Sands can't let you go. Let's get you to Command Hospital. You've been living with that pain in your chest for quite some time.'

'I've been living with pain my whole life, Aks. Without pain, I'd have been even more lost than I am.'

The doctors at Command Hospital recommended a short stay while they ran a series of tests. Kapo, General Bahadur, General Salman dropped in from time to time. Every morning and evening, Aks or his fiance Althea would bring some home-cooked food for him. Firebrand was at his grumpiest best. No one was bringing him his pouch of smokes or cigarettes despite his requests. 'What kind of a land is this? A Commander of 400,000 men, the architect of so many victories, and I can't even get a goddamn cigarette!'

When he was discharged, the doctors said he had angina and needed to stop smoking. Eat fruits, vegetables and fish, and no more beef, pork and lamb. The doctors recommended chicken but Firebrand dismissed the idea at once: 'That's two-legged. Doesn't work for me.' The doctors also advised rest for a while. There were medicines to be taken after meals. He needed to sleep well.

Back home, and sitting on the steps, he unconsciously rolled up a cigarette. Just as he was about to light it, someone coughed behind him. It was Marshal Rokossovsky.

'The doctors asked you not to smoke. But you've never been good with good advice.'

'I've come down to only six or seven a day.'

'FB, you have a problem listening to others.'

'Yes, I'm not good at taking orders.'

'Yet you insist yours be followed.'

'In war, yes.'

'Even otherwise: it's your way or the highway?'

'Not always.'

'More often than not. That's how you lost your family, isn't it?'

'We're not going there,' Firebrand snapped.

'You have anger issues—you're even shouting at a ghost.'

'Did you come here just to ruin my mood? I've been writing for the last few days and plan to get back to it.'

'As if the world of literature is waiting with bated breath for your shit.'

'You know, you're the most irritating ghost I've ever met.'

'As if you meet thousands every day.'

'Do you have anything to say, or are you just here to fry my brains?'

'I came for a chat. To be honest, no matter how obnoxious you are, I rather like you.'

'I'm flattered.'

'So, what do you think will happen now? Are you guys going to have your little country?'

'I don't know. But with annoying ghosts and talking animals on our side, I'll say we stand a fair chance.'

'You're still confused by all of this, aren't you?'

'Wouldn't you be?'

'Your grooming tells you all this is hyperreality. You're confused as hell. Your years of faith in your political beliefs, in the premise of rationality, have all been challenged. That was the last pillar you were leaning on, especially because all the others have crumbled away.'

'You're wrong. I was never that kind of an idiot. You guys were. That's why, for a good ten years, the land of Gogol and Bulgakov became famous for its mafia and whores.'

'Oh, you think so?'

'Yes, because the interpretation of an inherently human and idealist philosophy was so banal, and its implementation so cruel and so devoid of the human touch. You were pulled out of the Gulag to win the war. And after the war, when you became the Defence Minister of Poland, you sent more than 200,000 men to labour camps where a thousand died on the first day.'

'That's a broad and layered topic. How else do you think it ought to have been done after Lenin's death?'

'You can really get on someone's nerves, you know.'

'Your thinking is muddled. On the one hand, you don't want to believe in anything extra-human. On the other, your reality is not letting you rubbish it either.'

'You're a ghost but not a mind reader. Even the Soviet Union carried out extensive research on extra-sensory perception, clairvoyance and telepathy. I do concede there're things in this universe still beyond the reach of the human mind.'

'What's your take on God?'

'I don't know but I can say this much: that even your Stalin, the architect of the five-year plans of atheism, changed his stance towards the Church. He met Orthodox hierarchs too towards the middle of the war, no? Twelve priests blessed the soldiers guarding the Moscow lines from triple-seater Ishak fighters before the great pushback to Berlin began.'

'You think he really believed in all that? He did that merely to lift the soldiers' morale.'

'Even so, he did have to take recourse to God. He had to concede that the idea of God was a more powerful motivational factor in the mid-1940s, almost three decades after the revolution, than the dream of a utopian, egalitarian society. So, either God was stronger or the 30 years of Bolshevism, mostly under Stalin, was too weak. Or maybe the concept of God gives more strength than the zeal for establishing an equal society. How the hell will a stupid bozo like me know? I see one of my men falling. The next one says a prayer, trembling in fear, and picks up the first man's gun. Do I tell him, "Hey, you know what? You can't do that? That's fucking unscientific." There is a reason why after the war ended, the number of Orthodox churches in the Soviet Union had swelled from 400 in 1940 to over 22,000.'

'Why do you think that happened?'

'Hope. Hope keeps us ticking. When everything else fails, we turn to God for hope. It's our last resort. So do you. Millions of your soldiers wore symbols, chains and amulets under their undergarments, drew crosses on their vests before they went to die. Only two things spurred them on towards their end: their trust in their god, and their love for Mother Russia. Your system did not give them hope—it only gave them fear. A system that needs to kill millions to stay alive and stake its claim to be the torchbearer of an idealist, humane and equal society—such a system is incapable of spreading hope. That's the void where God steps in, with hope in the face of despair.'

'But you don't pray?'

'Driven to my wit's end at one point in my life, I too have knocked on his doors. He didn't hear me—so I stopped pestering him. Since then, I've never had any reason to go back to him. He's a busy person. So many prayers to listen to, maybe even answer. I'm sure mine slipped through his fingers. It happens.'

'And that's why you've developed this defence mechanism. This switch at will between existing and nothingness—'

'I *am* nothing. There is nothing after me, there was nothing before. I *am* insignificant. Merely awake for a while on this plane of consciousness. The day I feel I can't keep my eyes open any more, I'll pack up and go to sleep. At times, I have felt like forcing that sleep to come. But now I think I'll let it come when it will. It makes life unpredictable. And fun. Miserable fun, but fun all the same. By the way, I was planning to cook up some spicy beef curry for lunch. How would you like some with rice?'

'Good idea. I see you're not giving up red meat.'

'Yes. What tomorrow brings, I do not know. But right now, I know my red-hot beef curry, Kerala-style, will do me a world of good.'

'You make that and I'll get some real vodka, not this shit, and be right back. By the way, Firebrand, did you know: Stalin was not all that fond of vodka?'

'Yes, he liked brandy. Do you know what Hitler's poison was?'

'No, some wine perhaps.'

'No, nothing. He never drank any alcohol.'

'No wonder he lost the war,' giggled Marshal Rokossovsky as he walked out into the garden and disappeared into a shaft of sunlight.

XXVII

It did not take long for the bugles of war to sound again. The United Nations tried to intervene, but Bum said that the lives of WI citizens were at stake. He had credible intel that the captured military personnel were in immediate danger, that they had been forced to give those statements to the press and pose for the camera. His Press Secretary reported that the PRC command had threatened to sexually torture all the captured women soldiers if the Commanders did not publicly announce the defection of the Task Force fleet. The international community could go to hell if it wanted to, snarled Bum. Surely the UN would not forget that the WI was the single largest financial contributor to the world body?

Three fleets were sent to the aid of Connoway's Pacific Fleet. That made it 4 supercarriers and 70 missile cruisers, destroyers, corvettes and submarines, a mighty force by any standard. With 4 of the 11 supercarriers having defected along with the only one of the Republican Navy, it promised to be a good match. The Republican Navy sent 2 of its mammoth amphibious attack platforms with 12,000 well-trained troops each, apart from tanks and infantry fighting vehicles. The plan: to overwhelm the enemy with total air domination, and a severe pounding from the skies from heavy bombers. The ships had to be taken out first. Then the landing forces could be sent in. That was the overwhelming consensus at the Trapezium.

But General Norman Fornlopp, who was given the joint command of the operation, was against landing forces in Sands and the Seven Hills. 'You do not want to fight a resistance war in a land of 130 million with strong guerrilla military credentials,' he said in meeting with Bum and his top three aides.

'So, what do you propose, General?'

'We do it in pieces. We break it down. And we try to force a situation on the people where they rebel against their leaders.'

'Could you elaborate?'

'The first phase involves setting up proper bases in a little island about 20 miles north of Sands. We send people into Sands, in many disguises—as businessmen, as musicians, as technicians. I need the agency's cooperation here,' Fornlopp looked at Liz, who nodded. 'We locate potential targets aggrieved by this guerrilla regime and hand over to them the task of recruiting potential foot soldiers. We create a counter-guerrilla force, train them on this island and then send them back in. We create chaos and mayhem while our military operations continue alongside. Sooner or later, they will implode.'

'Just a point here,' said Liz, 'We're in touch with a few such people already. But they're not that influential.'

'Good. The less prominent, the better for us,' said Fornlopp.

'So, the first step is to take this island, right?' said Shane, 'How? The Pacific Fleet's movement is being monitored by their navy.'

'We have to paradrop our airborne forces. The Republic's Para Forces will join the operation as well. While they sanitize the area and establish bases in the forests, we engage their navy. We will take losses. But we can replenish quickly. They can't. Then we step up our bombing runs on the mainland. During war, imports get pricier. Goods and services become more expensive. People are not happy. There are regular bomb blasts in refineries, mines, tourist areas. Our recruits will be a thorn in their flesh. Businesses will start to pull back. Then we move to Stage 2.'

'General, if I may interrupt,' said Frank. 'You are aware of our pilots being force-landed by flying saucers. You obviously don't believe that horseshit, right?'

'Do I look like a superstitious fool? I belong to the Army, not your pampered naval cadre. It's obvious they were under pressure to come up with all that mumbo jumbo. Mr President has already clarified that we have the necessary intel.'

'Good to know. We also know they're waiting for the right moment to bite back,' said Bum.

'By the way, General, a part of the PRC fleet is moving north towards the island as we speak. It's a substantial force with three supercarriers,' Shane suddenly spoke up, his eyes glued to his phone screen.

'Mr President, sir, with your permission, I'd like to kickstart Operation Moby Dick.'

'You may, General.'

'Best of luck, General. Or should I call you Captain Ahab?' laughed Liz.

'Who's Captain Ahab?' was Bum's first question the moment Fornlopp was gone.

Both Shane and Liz were so nonplussed by the President's ignorance that they could say nothing for a few moments.

Frank stepped in. 'A fictional character, Bummer.'

'Oh! Fiction. I wonder why people read fiction. It has absolutely no use. I can understand self-help books or "better sex" books. But fiction! Anyway, do you think we should have told Fornlopp about the missing equipment, about Limpdick's crazy outburst? God only knows what more awaits us.'

'Absolutely not,' said Frank, 'He's a four-star General. Let him sort it out.'

That afternoon, missives went out to the command head-quarters of the 101 and 102 Airborne Divisions of the WI Army and the Parachute Regiment of the Republican Army: Be ready in 24 hours.

Bum had gone home early that day. He had to be ready for the President's Press Dinner. Over the last three years, he had not attended even one. But the way the press was going, Frank had advised him to be present this year and shake hands and play nice. 'You can't antagonize them any more, Bummer. Especially not after the revolt in the military.'

'So I have to bow down to that pack of sissy wolves? I've already said the prisoners admitted to all that stuff under pressure.'

'They're not buying that. You have to show up, share a few drinks, crack a few jokes, show them you're in control. And we'll be screening a short film on the importance of the free press, a PR exercise. You're in it too. Get in there, and keep smiling.'

Bum walked into the Round Hall ballroom that evening in a black tuxedo and shiny pointed shoes, stiff from the word go. But he managed to be courteous and restrained, and shook hands with a few of the journalists. A little later, everyone settled down and the film began. A shot of Bum, sitting in his office, waxing eloquent on the gallant role of the World Island press. Suddenly, the screen went dark. And then a message appeared: 'Exclusive footage from top-secret meetings. Get your cameras ready.' And a few seconds later, the conversation between Bum, Frank, Shane and Liz about the disappearance of wartime-reserve equipment began to play.

Pandemonium broke out. Frank ran to the projection room upstairs but found the door locked. The security guys punched in the code but the door was jammed. It took them a full seven minutes to break it down. By then, Limpdick's delirium had also been played on the screen downstairs, complete with Bum and Frank's interjections.

Editors and bureau heads began to call their offices and send in their recordings. In less than 10 minutes, every single TV station was beaming the footage out into the world.

When Frank and the guards finally broke down the door, the projection man was found unconscious, feathers stuffed into his mouth and nostrils. Frank turned towards the sliding window to the right. It was open. Three ospreys were sitting on the sill. One turned its head, winked at him and then they all flew away.

Downstairs, the film had come to an end. In place of the credits, some lyrics frozen on screen:

'There was a loony Dodi, and a crazy Bum
When one would rattle, the other would hum
One tiny piece of land, it made them so glum
When the scores are settled, it'll be the end of the sum.'

XXVIII

Seven nights before the meeting between Fornlopp and Bum, Firebrand was walking the same stretch which his old man had walked every evening about 40 years ago, on his way to buy his daily bottle of booze. The Jadavpur Foreign Liquor Shop used to be one of the only two shops in the area. In those days, colourful bottles did not sparkle under brash neon lights in the house of pints seven days a week. Low-powered yellow bulbs used to emit a timid glow. On Thursdays, when liquor stores across Sands were closed, there would be no light at all.

Firebrand walked past the shop and stopped about 50 metres away from the Pirbaba Mazar where the faithful lit candles every evening. A few homeless people clustered near the entrance, asking for alms. Firebrand sat on a rock on the footpath. The large tree behind him cast a dark shadow around the spot. He had walked for 15 minutes and was exhausted. An eight-storey apartment complex stood on the other side. Many years ago, from a taxi-repair shop at the same spot, Sebastian the Anglo-Indian had run his bootlegging operation. So, on Thursdays, or other 'dry days' such as Independence Day or a religious festival, people would come there to quench their thirst. Sebastian would keep the bottles hidden in the bonnets and boots of the cars. As the evenings rolled into nights and the city's gentry locked their doors shut, in every nook and corner of Calcutta, its dark underbelly would stir alive at its bootlegging vends. The city would metamorphose into a giant stage. A mega Rabelaisian carnival would unfold. As the bottle count went up, in the eyes and minds of the drunks, the streets transformed into rivers, the cars with their headlights became long-lost ferries looking for their anchors, the double-decker buses became dragons with glowing eyes, looking for prey. The empty white plastic packets thrown up into the air by a sudden gust of wind turned into gulls swooping into the ocean of the night.

There were those two old men who never spoke to anyone but each other. They played chess and left at the clockstrike of midnight. There were serious forms of gambling too. Frequent brawls, knife fights and the occasional gun shot. Then the cops would swarm all over the place. Sebastian and his customers would run helter-skelter. Bottles were loaded into sacks and dumped in the pond at the back of the garage only to be pulled back up after the cops had disappeared.

Firebrand was adrift on a ship of nostalgia—remembering the obnoxious games such as shoot-the-distance pissing contests, guess the next car's number plate—when a shabbily dressed man came up and stopped by his side. 'Can I sit down?

'Yes, of course,' said Firebrand, attempting to stand. 'I was just about to leave.'

'Don't go, not yet. I have a lot to tell you. Just move a little to the side. This rock is big enough for both of us.'

Firebrand shifted a little to one side. The man sat down and stuck out his right hand. 'Marshal Bhodi is my name.'

Firebrand was taken aback. 'I am—'

'I know. Who doesn't? Can any son of a cunt in this land say they haven't heard of General Firebrand? I am Marshal Bhodi. *Marshal.* I'm senior.'

'I—'

'You thought I was a figment of your old man's imagination. No?' Bhodi grinned, and Firebrand could see his tobacco-stained teeth.

'Yes, kind of.'

'Sebastian's place, huh! The boss used to come here. What fun this city once was,' Bhodi nudged Firebrand while staring in awe at the apartment complex and its ornate balconies.

'Yes, Dad used to come here. On Thursdays, or if he wanted to drink some more late at night.'

'I have a bottle of rum with me. You'll have some, won't you?'

'Yes, I could do with some free booze.'

Bhodi broke into loud laughter as he turned the cap of the bottle. 'Like father, like son. It's good to meet you. You do realize we're brothers, right?' He brought out two paper glasses and a bottle of water from the bag on his shoulder.

'Brothers?'

'Your father created me, after all. Had he not written his books, I wouldn't be here. Neither would Civet Cat or that crazy father of mine. Why did your father have to make that coprolalic raven my father, I have absolutely no idea!' Bhodi handed Firebrand his drink.

'OK, my long-lost brother, cheers,' said Firebrand.

'Cheers.'

'You don't like Raven, huh?'

'You can't not like your father. But he's got such a foul mouth, such a foul temper. And he's constantly putting me down in front of my wife.'

They talked endlessly for the next two hours. Rather, Firebrand did. From the role of the gold coin in world literature to Thor Heyerdahl's 1947 *Kon-Tiki* raft expedition, from the ghost of Warren Hastings at the National Library to the 80s project of mating tigers and lions to produce tigons for the Calcutta Zoo, from the fast-paced life of Davnagar to the absolute nothingness of the barren Zanskar Valley. He hadn't talked so much in years.

After he was done with the last two pours and thrown the bottle away on a heap of garbage a little distance away, Marshal Bhodi suddenly grew emotional. Firebrand found it a bit silly. But, then, that's what drunken conversations are about. Everything in life need not have a purpose.

Firebrand was also feeling very, very sleepy.

'You've had an interesting life, General.'

'Yes, it's been pretty eventful.'

'Most people have mundane lives. Like a placid lake. They go to school, then university. Then a job, a wife, a house, maybe a car. Some build businesses, buy Learjets and banks.'

'Hmm.'

'And they fuck and procreate. Their children go through the same grind. And then they get fat and die. The next generation, already going through the same fucking cycle, organizes condolence meetings in their memory and prints their pictures in the newspapers.'

'Sounds like a good life.'

'Nope, sounds like a waste to me. They leave nothing behind. Nothing that lasts. Nothing people will remember them by, except the photographs on the walls of their children.'

'I don't think anyone will have my picture on their wall after I'm gone.'

'Oh, wait and watch, General. You'll see.'

'When? Soon?'

'Can't tell. But you'll see. Nothing that lasts comes without pain, without loss, without insecurity, without fear, without brashness, without emotions, without turmoil, without courage, without madness.'

'I didn't sign up for this, you know. I wanted a simple life, a home full of people to come back to. See my son grow up into a fine, young man. Fall asleep knowing the person lying next to me is the one I love and I am the one she loves.'

'You were not supposed to have that life, that's what normal Johnnies have. That has never been your destiny.'

'I had it all but I fucked it up. I think I became General Firebrand to escape Roy's predicament. I have to go now. I'm very sleepy and I'm talking shit. I haven't drunk this much in a while. I'm sorry. I don't know how I'll get back home.'

'Take a rickshaw. You're in no position to walk. Sleep well. The war's coming again, and Sands can't afford to have General Firebrand short of sleep.'

'I'm tired of fighting. I'm just too goddamn tired. I can't take a rickshaw. I've left my wallet at home.'

'Leave that to me.'

Marshal Bhodi held Firebrand's arm and tottered to the rickshaw stand at the Lord's Bakery crossing. With help from the rickshaw puller, he managed to lift Firebrand onto the seat.

'Take him to his house in Golf Green. Next to C. S. Park. Ground floor, left-hand side when you make the right from Lover's Lane. How much?'

'Twenty, sir.'

'Take extra, but get him home.'

'Yes, sir. His face looks familiar. Is he an actor?'

'Have you heard of General Firebrand?'

'Oh! Is that him? I'll make sure I get him home, sir. You don't have to pay me.'

'No, he won't like that. And he'd like it if you kept the extra 10 bucks. This is what he's been fighting for. Get him home safely. Make sure he goes in.'

Fifteen minutes later, as Firebrand lay sprawled in his parents' bedroom on the very bed where he and Laila had once been in each other's arms, his cell phone rang.

'Hello . . . '

'Marshal Bhodi here. Just wanted to make sure you were home.'

'I just want to sleep. Leave me alone.'

'You still have one good fight left in you, brother. Your father watches over you. So does your mother. Don't let them down. This is not the time to give up. Goodnight.'

The phone slipped from Firebrand's hands as he rolled deeper and deeper into an endless pit. Soft and thick, the coils of sleep pulled him towards the very heart of blackness.

The blue Buddha on the bookshelf above the bed kept vigil until it grew light.

XXIX

Five days before half of Sands' naval fleet set sail for the island's northeastern coast, a large number of small boats and barges had left Devil's Lair for the southern coasts of the Island of Bald Mountain. About 24 hours later, Colonel Abbas with his 2,000 special-forces personnel and Colonel Aks with his 2,000 super-infantry commandos were at the beaches. It had been a noon landing. General Firebrand arrived at night. Under cover of darkness, 8,000 battle-hardened men of the 1st Strike Corps got off and began to unload their equipment. The boats carried the men, and the barges the small field artillery, heavy machine guns, anti-material rifles, mortars, shoulder-fired anti-air missiles, rocket launchers, landmines and vast quantities of ammunition. The 12,000-strong force stayed for the night in the jungle that began just 150 metres from the coastline.

Early the next morning, Firebrand was on the beach, swimming along the shore with an energy that could only be compared to the second hand of a self-winding watch. He got tired after a only a few minutes, though, and was panting heavily when he felt a gentle hand on his back. It was Marshal Rokossovsky. He had three men with him, whom he introduced to Firebrand. They shook hands, and then Rokossovsky asked, 'So General, what are your plans?

'Let's talk over some coffee,' said Firebrand and gestured for them to follow him into the jungle. Once they were in front of his tent, Firebrand requested a soldier for four cups of coffee.

'Elan does not drink coffee,' said Olga.

'Neither does the Khan,' said the Marshal.

'Tea, then,' asked Firebrand.

'I'll try coffee,' said the Khan. Olga spoke to Elan in some strange tongue and returned. 'Elan won't have anything.'

Once the coffees arrived, Firebrand picked up a large twig and began to draw an outline of the island on the ground.

'First, with a 30-plus warship cordon with air cover, I rule out naval landings till our fleet is standing. Now, this island is surrounded by a dense jungle on three sides: the south, the east and the west. In some places, it starts no further than 50 metres from the water. It makes landing paratroopers in these locations next to impossible, the trees are too tall and close together. Rappelling from choppers is possible but it would take an unusually high number of helos.'

'All right, go on,' said the Marshal.

'But towards the north, 4 kilometres in front of this brown mountain, there is a lagoon.'

Olga butted in. 'It's the Bald Mountain. This is the Island of Bald Mountain.'

'I see. The beachhead there is nearly 450 metres from the nearest vegetation. Between the lagoon and the Bald Mountain, this 4-kilometre stretch has many hillocks. It's bushy terrain, pretty dense but not many large trees. About 2 kilometres wide.

'It's here that the bastards will try to paradrop their troopers. I intend to set up a ring around this zone. To make sure they can't consolidate at the centre, I want to put up gun positions on these hillocks. They can sanitize the area around them from a height, and the forces on the perimeter can concentrate on ground-level fire. That will also ensure that my boys and girls don't fall to friendly fire.'

'Sounds good, General.'

'But to offset select Special Forces landings from the sea around the island and abseiling from choppers behind our lines, I'd like to set up some outposts all along the coast and in the jungle. And I'd want this stretch of the beach in front of the lagoon to be mined.'

'You don't need to worry about these coasts and the jungle. His forces will be in the forest, all along the coastline, to take care of our unwanted guests,' said the Marshal pointing to the Khan.

'Whose forces?' asked Firebrand.

'The Mongol Army, builders of the largest empire known to mankind before the advent of the Industrial Revolution,' said the Khan with pride.

Firebrand was bewildered. Marshal Rokossovsky said, 'The name is Chengiz Khan. He is the Khan of the Khans.'

Firebrand stared for a few seconds at the bearded man who looked more like a Confucian saint than the founder of the fabled Mongol Empire. 'I seriously hope they don't try anything like that. I wouldn't wish even my worst enemy to confront a Mongol ghost army inside a forest.'

'Let's prepare to leave, General. It's a long way from here,' said the Marshal.

The PRC force was divided into three. While the majority of the troopers was to trek through the forests in two lines on opposite banks of a creek that ran through the length of the island and ended in the jungle just behind the Bald Mountain, Elan and his men would ferry the rest on their small country boats. From where the creek ended, which was five kilometres from the lagoon, the soldiers would cart the heavy equipment to their positions.

Olga and Marshal Rokossovsky led the way for the column of troops on the left bank. Chengiz Khan and a few of his Mongol warriors took responsibility of the foot party on the right. Firebrand took the waterway.

Tall trees crowded onto the creek from either side. Some of them, especially the coconuts and the palms, reached out to one another like lovers attempting a final kiss, creating a canopy over the waters. From their boats, Firebrand and Elan could occasionally glimpse the troops walking along the banks. Hear them rustling to and fro, carrying their equipment, sometimes even a snatch of a song.

The narrow boats slid through the water like knives. Occasionally, snakes hanging from the overhead branches would drop into the boats. They were tossed into the water. Once in a while, a crocodile floated past, suspiciously calm. Even though this was the swiftest and smoothest way to transport their heavy weapons, it would be two days before Firebrand and his men arrived at the end of the creek.

At night, they drew close to the bank and pitched their tents. Elan's men lit fires and took turns to stand guard to keep the crocodiles from sidling ashore and snatching away one of the men. The troops, tired from the hauling and loading and unloading, would fall asleep in minutes. Firebrand would sit outside his tent for a while, fiddling with his ukulele. Then he'd get into his tent, and fall at once into a dreamless sleep.

XXX

It must have been around 8 p.m., three evenings after the men had alighted from their boats, when General Firebrand, guided by Talking Crane, entered the crater on the top of the Bald Mountain. The Hollow was reverberating with laughter and animated conversation. Aurelio, Sitaram and Olga, Marshal Zhukov, Marshal Rokossovsky, Marshal Malinovsky, Marshal Bagramyan, Civet Cat, Raven, Begum Johnson, Vasily Zaitsev and the snipers, Chengiz Khan and four of his Mongol Generals—they were all there. As was a lot of date wine and three whole roasted pigs.

Rokossovsky introduced Firebrand to everyone and Aurelio handed him an earthen bowl of drink. He went through three pours very quickly and was gradually losing his politeness when Raven flew over and landed next to him.

'Dondobayosh here. I guess you've already met my incorrigible son. He must have bad-mouthed me as usual. Didn't he?'

'Yes, we had a good time. No, he didn't say anything terrible about you.'

'No one can have a good time with that waster. Can you believe it? He calls himself Marshal. Look at these men.

Zhukov, Rokossovsky, Malinovsky . . . If they are Marshals, how dare that scumbag Bhodi call himself one?'

'I guess Marshal Bhodi is getting hauled over the coals for my old man's fault. My father's the one who gave him the title.'

'How would he have known? Men like Bhodi should be kept on a whiplash.'

'As a father, I don't think Spartan discipline does any good to one's child.'

'I'm old school. Spare the rod, spoil the child.'

Firebrand was about to say something when a nasal voice piped up from his right: 'I'm really impressed by your planning and meticulous execution, General.'

Firebrand had not realized that Marshal Zhukov had walked up to him.

'I try to do what I think is best, Marshal. At times, it works. At times, it doesn't.'

'You go by your instinct. It has never been the brain or the heart that has won wars. It's always instinct. And that is what sets one General apart from the others. Rokossovsky's told me all about you. I wish you many more victories.'

Firebrand needed some air. He put down the earthen bowl and walked up, back to the entrance at the top. Outside, he lit a cigarette and stared at the vast expanse in front, leading up to the lagoon. His boys and girls were already in position, and the beach had been heavily mined. His men had worked only at night, thus evading detection. During the day, they'd hidden in the forests while their machine guns and other heavy weaponry on the hillocks had been camouflaged by branches and trees.

By the light of the moon, the white sands of the lagoon gleamed like a silver necklace. He could see movement around some of the machine-gun and mortar positions in the bushes on the hillocks. And occasional lighter flashes among the troopers assembled on the edges of the jungle. From a distance, they looked like fireflies. Beyond the white sands, where lay the still waters of the green lagoon, there was darkness. He turned to go back into the crater, and found Sitaram standing there. Firebrand had not heard a thing. Sitaram had arrived in silence.

Firebrand said a polite hello and was about to walk past when Sitaram caught hold of his hand. Firebrand looked at him. The look in Sitaram's eyes was unnerving, as if the tantric's eyes were piercing right through him, looking into his soul.

'You must tread carefully, soldier.'

'Thanks. Yes, it is pretty uneven here. I'll be careful.'

'You must watch your step. Always. Be mindful when you walk, soldier.'

Firebrand went back into the Hollow. He was hungry. He drank no more but quickly devoured almost a kilo of the delicious pork. Then he said his goodbyes and started to trek back to his position, around 500 metres from the shoreline on the first hillock. As he trudged down the turnpikes, the violin crescendo of Modest Mussorgsky's *Night on Bald Mountain* began to play inside his head. He started humming as he walked.

It was almost midnight when he reached his command centre. Talking Crane, who accompanied him, wished him luck and flew away. He checked on the radio about the positions of his various teams, spoke to the communications officers on board the lead ship of the Sands naval fleet. 'As soon as our radars pick up anything, we'll relay it to you,' came the assuring reply from SNS *Awakening*.

He must have slept for about two and a half hours when the radio began to crackle. It was Admiral Limpdick himself. 'Our fleet has moved into the high seas to engage the WI ships. We're picking up heavy- and medium-lift transports headed for the island, escorted by fighters. Godspeed, General. I've passed on the info to Captain Roy as well. You will soon have air support.'

'How far, Admiral?'

'Any time now, General. Any time.'

Firebrand switched radio frequencies and spoke to his commanders. The teams loaded their weapons and got into alert positions.

The radio buzzed again. 'Captain Roy here. We're taking off. This is your night. The night of the General. Give them hell.'

Firebrand stood up for one last smoke before action. The water in the lagoon was calm. There were no sounds except for the cocking of weapons, of magazines sliding into the guns, of rockets locking themselves into their launchers. A gentle breeze was blowing. 'No matter what the outcome, this will be one night the sands and the stones of the Island of Bald Mountain will remember for a long time to come,' Firebrand thought to himself as he exhaled.

In the Hollow, everyone had just finished their late dinner when Aurelio shouted, 'It's time. Let's move to the gallery. The show's about to begin.'

'I have to go now,' said the Khan.

'Khan, stay with us,' said Rokossovsky, 'I'm sure your Generals can handle the situation.'

The Great Khan waved at his four Generals; they all followed him out of the crater and disappeared into the darkness.

With Sitaram and Aurelio leading the way, the other guests gathered outside on the flat rock that looked out at the lagoon. 'The best position to see a battle from,' Rokossovsky shouted. Zaitsev and his sniper buddies said they wanted to join the fight. They started running down the mountain.

'You fought when it was your time. Let them fight theirs now. It's your time to watch,' yelled a drunk Zhukov.

'You lot are the Marshals and Generals. You can afford to watch. I'm a soldier. I can't sit back,' Zaitsev screamed back.

'To the camp or the firing squad?' Zhukov asked Malinovsky with a frown.

'Does it make any difference?' replied Malinovsky.

'What do you mean?' Zhukov shot back.

Rokossovsky butted in: 'Marshal, you are way too drunk. Vasily is long dead and gone. Your Gulags or firing squads can't destroy his spirit any more.'

'No more bitterness. No more quarrels. Here's to the last lull before the storm,' said Aurelio who'd brought a pitcher of date wine with him.

They settled down on the rock.

Soon, their voices could no longer be heard. The sonic boom of the jet engines roared and ripped through the air around Bald Mountain.

XXXI

In all honesty, Admiral Limpdick had miscalculated badly and ventured too far into the deep sea to pursue the WI fleet which was drawing further and further back. That was exactly the tactic that Admiral Connoway had communicated to General Fornlopp: 'Dicky's a hunter. He loves to chase his prey. I'll lure him out into the deep waters as far away from the island as possible. The aircraft carrying our airborne troops will be out of his anti-air missile range. If he sends his combat planes after them, he'll end up thinning out his own air cover. That's when my planes will strike.'

'What if he doesn't send them and engages you instead?'

'Even better. Our men will take the island without any resistance.'

'And your fleet?'

'Let's just say the better Admiral of the two will be left standing.'

Fornlopp had planned to drop about 5,000 men onto the island but was not so sure any more. Even though the island was unprotected, he hesitated to commit his entire force at one go. In case the PRC had even a small presence hidden there, it would be good if he had men on hand to clean up the area while reinforcements arrived. He'd also planned to land some specially trained Walrus forces on the beaches towards the west and east; they could come through the forests, cleansing any resistance in their way. He had chosen 30 landing spots where teams of 12 could land in their 2-men minisubs. They could exfil the same way, and be picked up by WI submarines.

In the end, he decided to paradrop 3,000 soldiers in the first wave, and 2,000 later, also airborne and closely following the first party. Accordingly, the airborne soldiers had gathered at their respective stations from where they were flown to the massive WI military base at Don Diego in the middle of the Indian Ocean.

Finally, 5,000 paratroopers took off from Don Diego in 90 C-130 Hercules transporters. Their drop zone was 2 hours away. Almost 48 hours ago, the Walrus operatives had departed Don Diego in more than 20 submarines; about 50 nautical miles from the shores of the Bald Mountain, the amphibian forces left the main vessels in their minisubs and prepared to land on the beaches.

As Fornlopp was fairly certain that there was no or scanty presence of PRC forces on the ground, he went for high-altitude low-opening jumps. The hatches of more than 50 C-130 Hercules opened up and 3,100 paratroopers jumped out and fell free at terminal velocity till they were a kilometre from the surface of the Island of Bald Mountain; then they opened their parachutes.

Upon orders from General Firebrand, troops on the hillocks and the edges of the jungle let off more than 100 flares, and the gunners on the ground opened fire. Many of the airborne troops were riddled by bullets before they touched the ground. Those who did touch the ground found themselves in a literal minefield. Those who landed between the lagoon and the mountain came under heavy fire from the top of the hillocks as well as the perimeter that circled the drop zone. Within 15 minutes of landing, the airborne troops had already lost more than 800 men. Around 700 more lay injured, slowly bleeding to death.

Colonel Larry Bing sent out an immediate SOS for air support, and a warning to hold the next wave of paratroopers. His men relayed the coordinates of the enemy's positions to the fighter escorts who let go off some of their precision ground bombs and missiles. The first salvo was massive, and Firebrand saw the edges of the forests aflame and three of his hill positions blown to smithereens.

The exchange of fire was becoming more and more desperate when General Firebrand and Colonel Bing suddenly spotted countless lights zipping across the sky towards the WI fighters. Laddie and Hobgoblin had arrived with their flying saucers!

As the WI jet fighters were engaged by the saucers in impossible dogfights, Firebrand's men started closing in on the invading forces from the edge of the forests while the gun positions rained hell on them from the tops and edges of the hillocks.

The WI pilots soon ran out of their air-to-air missiles. They had not hit a single saucer. Now it was back to the old way: the gun. But the saucers went on the offensive, attacking the jet outlets, their razor-sharp edges cutting across them before crashing into the engines. Some went for the wings and sliced them off. The pilots had no option but to bail. By the time they hit land, the operations on the ground had come to an end: Colonel Bing had surrendered with his men to the PRC forces. The pilots who landed on the island had been captured. The fabled WI air force had just lost 60 of its top-of-the-line combat jets. Laddie and Hobgoblin had concentrated on the departing unarmed C-130 Hercules transporters, and managed to shoot down as many as 30.

General Firebrand allowed Colonel Bing to speak to his superior officer. General Fornlopp retired to his room in shock at the Don Diego military base. He took off the cross he wore around his neck, hung it on his family photograph, said a prayer, pulled out his service pistol and blew his brains out.

Colonel Bing and his men, 1,500 of them including the injured, were surrounded by PRC soldiers in the middle of the drop zone. Those who were not wounded came forward, five at a time, and surrendered their weapons. In the meantime, the three medic companies embedded with Firebrand's forces had started attending to the injured from both sides.

Though he had won the battle, General Firebrand was grim: more than 500 of his boys and girls lay dead, and over 400 were injured.

Major Gurung, commander of the medic battalion, came up to Firebrand. 'General, some of the soldiers need immediate surgery. We will try to do our best but they need to be evacuated as fast as possible. The numbers are too overwhelming for my team. The injured can't travel across the forests to the southern tip. They have to be evacuated from the north beach itself.'

Firebrand got in touch with Kapo. A few helicopters were allocated to fly out the most seriously injured. The boats and barges which had returned to Sands after dropping Firebrand and his men had set sail already, and would arrive on the northern shores, off the beach by the lagoon, in 30 hours or so. In the meantime, of course, the beach had been heavily mined. It would need to be de-mined before people could walk across the beach and to the boats. Firebrand told the sappers that they needed to get into action early in the morning. 'It needed to be demined before we left anyway. There are people living in these forests, Kapo. Innocent people. We brought our war to their doorstep.'

'It'll take a long time, FB.'

'We will do it. Leave that to me. Over and out.'

Major Gurung's men performed surgeries non-stop in their portable operation theatres. Bing's troops had two platoons of medics, they worked without pause as well. But the numbers were simply overwhelming. All the injured were administered liberal dosages of morphine. 'This way, they won't die in pain. That's the least we can do,' Major Gurung told Captain Dr Ian Gooch of the WI Air Force who simply nodded.

Just before the break of dawn, Khan's Generals arrived with their prisoners: all 360 Walrus operatives, captured alive and disarmed. The Mongols had brought with them also the minisubs and all their weapons. The Walrus forces had been walking through the jungle for quite some time till they realized that their numbers were dwindling mysteriously. The Mongols, expert archers and swordsmen, did not have to resort to any of their fighting skills. The expert horsemen simply used their uurgas, a variant of the lasso but longer, to trip the WI men, lift them up into the trees before tying them up and gagging them and slinging them onto their horses.

By 9 a.m. the PRC leadership had decided to release photographs and videos of the captured soldiers and weapons to the international press. Brigadier Monet, the PRC Army spokesman, would read out the losses suffered by the invading forces. As proof, he would run the footage shot by Hobgoblin of a couple of C-130 Hercules being hit and catching fire in the air. The press conference was scheduled for four that afternoon.

The WI Secretary of Defence Shane Fairbanks had just eaten a late dinner at home on Saturday and was putting his younger son to bed when he received the call from the Trapezium. He did not say much. He hung up, kissed his son's forehead, turned off the lamp, came out of the room and called Frank Pollard.

'Mr Secretary, I need to see you.'

'When?'

'Now.'

'I'm out at a friend's place. It's an anniversary dinner. Can we meet tomorrow morning instead? Breakfast at my place, Shane?'

'I don't think so. I have to break this to the President. I want you there as well. I'm reaching his place in an hour.'

'He's not at his place, Shane. He's at Nancy's.'

'Then we go there. The bastard has fucked this country. He can fuck his whore a little later.'

'I'll meet you outside the building, Shane. Ten o'clock?'

'Yes.'

Shane hung up.

XXXII

President Bum was feeling his manhood grow inside Nancy's warm mouth when the doorbell rang. Nancy put on a robe and went to get the door. Bum muttered a series of expletives as he pulled up his trousers again.

'It's Frank and Shane. They say it's urgent.'

'I'm sorry, Nancy. It's not easy being President. I'll be right back.'

Shane and Frank left 10 minutes later. Nancy waited for a few minutes for Bum to come back to the bedroom. When he didn't, she walked out and found the President sitting on the sofa like a statue, looking up at the ceiling, lost in thought.

'What's the matter?'

The President put his arms around her and began to sob inconsolably. Quite a few minutes later, he lifted his head and asked for a drink. Nancy got up and poured him a large bourbon.

Bum took a few sips, then gulped down the rest. Then he got up: 'I'll be back in an hour. Put on the sexiest lingerie you've got and wait for me.'

He drove straight to the Trapezium and strode into the operations room. He spoke to the on-shift General who frantically called his superior officers.

On his way back to Nancy's apartment, Bum felt much better. When Shane and Frank told him that the paradrop had turned into a disaster, he had not been ready for the magnitude of the mess. Nearly 3,000 special-operations troops! 360 Walrus men! 60 fighter jets! 30 transporters! And the rout of the Pacific Fleet with its additional reinforcements had been the last nail in the coffin.

Admiral Connoway had thought he'd been playing Admiral Limpdick by drawing him out into the open seas. He had not realized that Admiral Limpdick was craftier. Before Limpdick set sail, he had dispatched Admiral Townsend, a career submariner, at the head of six of the stealth subs, to the east of Sands, going around the Seven Hills and further east to appear behind the Pacific Fleet. Limpdick himself sailed up the western coast of Sands.

Townsend had done what he was supposed to do: he appeared behind the Pacific Fleet which saw the sonar signatures, same as the other White Shark subs in the WI Navy, and was fooled into believing they were additional WI reinforcements. As a result, his submarines sent 12 high-powered torpedoes each at two of the supercarriers of Connoway's fleet. Both sank in less than two hours.

A barrage of 24 anti-ship cruise missiles had taken care of the two cruisers and four destroyers, the mainstay of the Pacific Fleet's anti-air capability. Connoway was in a quandary. On the one hand, he had to mount a major rescue mission to save the 12,000-odd floating sailors while he was floating around himself. On the other, Limpdick's fleet was closing in with three supercarriers and one carrier. Six of his escort submarines were chasing Townsend's underwater vessels. His fleet had nearly no anti-air missile batteries left.

The first thing Connoway did after he was pulled up from the seas was to establish radio contact with Admiral Limpdick. 'We are ready to surrender. What are your terms, Admiral?'

Limpdick met the surrendered fleet halfway and was escorting them back to Sands at the same time as Shane had been putting his child to bed.

Within 10 minutes of Bum leaving the Trapezium, the entire WI top brass had come to know: the President had ordered multiple nuclear strikes on Sands and the Seven Hills. To be executed within 12 hours.

Shane called Frank in disbelief. 'How do we stop this, Frank? This is madness.'

'You can't. I tried, but he hung up on me.'

Bum was whistling in the elevator as it carried him up to Nancy's 49th-floor apartment. He was in a good mood. As soon as Nancy opened the door in white satin and lace, he picked her up and practically ran to the bedroom. He cast away all pretensions of foreplay and tore off her scraps of delectable clothing, only to realize that he was not hard enough. So, as always, Nancy had to take the initiative and awaken Bum's little man. She kissed him on his mouth and slowly moved lower and lower . . . Bum was wriggling with pleasure when Nancy let out a terrifying scream. The President leapt to his feet and spun around to see a giant long-horned bird perched on the headboard. Its head almost touched the ceiling. Its beak was long, with fierce striations along the edges.

A naked Bum slowly tried to back away towards the door, holding Nancy in front of him, when the bird, with one swift movement of its long neck, brought its face between him and the door. 'Hiding behind the woman, are we?'

Nancy had passed out.

'Don't let her fall. Lay her down on the bed.'

Bum did as he was told.

'Good. Now call the nukes off.'

'What if I don't?'

'Well, I'll pick at your tiny pecker to begin with. Then I'll drill through your thick skull and eat your brains.'

'You fucking monster, you won't get away with this.'

'I'm only joking. You really think I'll touch that filthy dick of yours? And eat your brains? How can I eat something that does not exist? Now, listen carefully. You will also call your representative to the UN who will convene a Security Council meeting tomorrow morning at 9.30. She will make sure that the resolution for the independence of Sands and the Seven Hills is passed unanimously. The Secretary General must follow with an announcement to the press, confirming the same.

Then you will make a formal announcement, ending the war against Sands. Things should wrap up by 11 a.m. at the latest. Is that understood?'

'You are blackmailing the President of World Island. You've got no clue who you're fucking with.'

The long-horned bird brought its face even closer to Bum's and spoke in the coldest voice that the President had ever heard. 'You have no choice, Bum. If you do not do as you are instructed, then by 9.30 tomorrow the World Island's count of great cities will be down by one. And yes, I'll peck you to death as well. Slowly. Very slowly.'

Bum looked at the bird with dread. 'What do you mean?'

'I'll show you what I mean. You remember the Lunch Box bomb, Bum? Now open your e-mail.'

Bum froze in fear. So, that's what the buggers had been up to. He stumbled towards his trousers which were lying on the floor and pulled his mobile phone out of a pocket. He unlocked it and clicked on his email app.

'Open the one from Orion Crest.'

Bum clicked on the email. As it opened and he kept scrolling, he found himself going cold with fear.

The email had 12 pictures of the Lunch Box bomb placed in 12 of the largest cities of World Island. Each was home to at least 10 million people. The text read: 'The Lunch Box has been travelling across the length and breadth of your country before being placed in our desired destinations. Who knows where it is. It could be the Capital, it could be the City of No Sleep. It could be Crownpoint or the City of Seven Sins. The counter of the bomb corresponds to the time that this mail has been sent. Time is not on your side.'

The lone video attachment showed that the timer on the Lunch Box bomb had been turned on. There were 10 hours and 30 minutes to go. The mail had been sent at 11 p.m.

'Get up, you swine, and get to work,' said the bird.

The next half hour saw President Bum on the phone. After he got off the final call with Nida Dodi, who was predictably furious, he went back to his inbox. He wanted to forward it to Liz—but the email was not there. He even searched through the Trash folder, but it had vanished.

'The email's gone. How do we get the location of the bomb?'

'We get what we want first. Then you'll have your bomb back,' the big bird said before stalking off onto the terrace and taking off into the sky.

XXXIII

By the time Kapo caught Firebrand on the radio, it was late at night on the Island of Bald Mountain. Black Panther was sitting with El Comandante. He puffed on a cigar and El Comandante smoked his pipe. There were two glasses of rum on the table before them.

'We did it, FB,' Kapo said, 'Rather: you did it?'

'Since you are not here, you would have to credit me for the victory.'

'Not that victory, FB. We're an independent nation at last! The world has acknowledged it.'

'What, Kapo?'

Kapo brought Firebrand up to speed. The Security Council had passed a resolution in the City of No Sleep: its permanent members had all voted in favoured recognition of Sands and the Seven Hills as independent countries. The Secretary General had confirmed the same to the international media just a few hours ago.

President Bum called a press conference and announced the end of the war on Sands. He said he was looking forward to working with Sands and the Seven Hills on tackling global issues.

Firebrand could not hold back his relief. 'So many lives, Kapo! So many men and women. All for this one moment, this moment.'

'I know, FB. Come back soon. We haven't had a drink together in a decade.'

'As soon as I land in Calcutta, Kapo. I'll going to wake you up even if it's 3 a.m.'

'FB, you can wake me up any time. This would not have been possible without you. Black Panther told me everything. He's sitting with me right now.'

'What did that beast tell you?'

'That it was your idea to smuggle the bomb into World Island via that UN charter flight. In Ryan's luggage. Aks collected it once they landed. It worked. That Bum bastard had really readied his nukes for us. Your plan saved the day.'

'It was just my idea, Kapo. I told Marshal Rokossovsky. He must have organized its execution. I thought it might give us leverage in case the lunatic chose the mass-destruction route.'

'Just come back, FB. The war is over. Your house in the mountains, you remember? Any place you like.'

'There's been a slight change in plans. I'll tell you when I see you, Kapo. Over and out.'

Firebrand had been busy all day. There were a lot of dead men and women, and they had to be buried. The injured needed to be brought closer to shore. The sappers had been clearing the beach all the day. Since time was of the essence, they had marked off strips of sand leading up to the waters. That way, the soldiers could have a pathway along which to evacuate the wounded while the demining operation carried on elsewhere.

Firebrand had taken a walk around the island. He'd always wanted a place in the mountains, a small house with a garden where he could grow vegetables and flowers. The Island of Bald Mountain was not a bad spot at all. There was lush greenery. There were the emerald-green waters, the white-sand beach, the imposing brown mountain, the hillocks, the forest. He would be happy here . . . He could have a small motor boat to visit Sands whenever he felt like it. Here there seemed to be enough solitude to do his own thing, to write a few lines, to set them to tune, to have all the seafood that his doctors had prescribed. He did not need money here . . .

Marshal Rokossovsky and Chengiz Khan were standing on the beach, overseeing the demining operations. The sappers were worried that a day was too little time, that they would only be able to do a shoddy job of clearing the whole beach. Firebrand knew they were right, but had no solution to offer.

'Do you know,' said Marshal Rokossovsky, 'in the Great Patriotic War, when the Red Army was advancing, how we would clear the minefields—'

Firebrand gave him a caustic look. 'Yes, I know and I'm not doing anything like that here. Not using my own men, nor using the prisoners.'

'You don't understand me, do you? I am not asking your men to do it. But what about the Khan's men? They're already dead. Why not use them?'

Firebrand enveloped Marshal Rokossovsky in a tight hug. 'Brilliant idea! That's why I'm a General and you a Marshal.'

'Marshal is just a rank of honour, General. Deep inside, we're all mere Commanders who like to be in control.'

Within an hour, the entire beach had been cleared of all equipment and men as The Great Khan gathered his 200,000-strong ghost army and charged at the seas. As they trampled the sand all across the length and breadth of the beach, the mines exploded in their thousands.

Firebrand wanted a rerun of the same many times over just to be sure, but the sappers said that was not needed—nearly every square inch of the beach had been covered and cleared. At night, the ferries and boats would arrive, and they could all leave the island by the morning.

After President Bum addressed the press, he went to his office and sat in his chair. He called Naomie, his secretary, and was going through his engagements for the week when an osprey flew in through the open window and sat on his table. It carried a folded piece of paper in its beak. It tossed it towards Bum, shat on the table and flew away. Bum opened the short letter.

He read it and asked Naomie to leave. Then he put his head down on the table.

The note read:

Bummer Man,

We know we were supposed to tell you where the bomb is but we don't think we can trust you. All we can tell you is that it's safely stored and won't make a reappearance until you misbehave again.

Also, please do not stand for re-election. We would then have to release the videotape of the conversation between a naked you and Birdie at Nancy's joint. It won't show Birdie, just play his voice. We think you've fucked both the WI and the world enough in these four years. We would like to spare the people and this earth the horrific prospect of another four years of your antics.

Bye, Bummer,
You know who we are

The first light of dawn was filtering through the clouds when the loading of men and equipment was finally completed on the shores of the green lagoon in the Island of Bald Mountain. One by one, the boats began to leave. Firebrand climbed onto the last one. The engine man fired up the turbine. Suddenly Firebrand asked the man to stop for five minutes. He took off his boots, got into the water and started wading towards the beach. This was one place he did not want to leave. As his toes touched the sand on the beach, he shouted, 'I'm going but I'll be back.' He wanted one last smoke here, at this spot, looking out at the green water. He took out his cigarette case, brought out one of his hand-rolled cigarettes and lit up. He looked at the Bald Mountain. The brown hulk of rocks stood against the white of the sands and the green of the forest. What a place . . . He could picture his cabin, up there on one of the hillocks. He would have it on the first one from the shore that served as his command post. The flowerbed, the kitchen garden . . . Just a few more drags and he'd wade back to the boat, back to Calcutta, back to the independent country of Sands. But this was his place for sure. The Island of Bald Mountain. There was something about the name. It would make such a perfect address.

He took one last drag, flung the cigarette down on the sand and put out his right foot to stub it.

XXXIV

There was absolutely nothing even a seasoned hand like Firebrand could have done about it. The landmine exploded right under him and he was thrown a good at least 3 metres away. He somehow managed to pull himself up but his legs seemed to end at his knees. He felt as though his insides were being remoulded, as though his organs were being sucked out by a giant vacuum cleaner, being thrashed by heavy pistons. He convulsed for a few seconds. Then he felt light, as light as a gas balloon. He couldn't see. He couldn't speak, couldn't feel. Just two faces flashed through the light. Ryan and Lai. Laughing faces, happy faces. And a smell, that intoxicating, ethereal smell of Lai's skin. Then General Firebrand fell. He fell flat on his face. He felt absolutely nothing any more ever again.

Roy's mother was preparing a meal. The pressure cooker whistled every few minutes or so. It smelt like mutton. Roy's father, with his trademark beard, was seated on his side of the table, in front of two now-empty coffee cups, and taking his insulin shot. His writing pad was lying open at the table's corner, with a pen on top. Roy was reading a book in which a peasant wrote letters to God for a good harvest. His mother came and put a tray with four baked tilapias on the table. Roy's playwright grandfather was on the veranda, feeding the numerous birds on their perches. A squirrel was having its customary mashed potato.

Roy's mother called out to his grandfather. 'Baba, come for lunch. Roy is back home after so long. Let's all eat together. Roy, put the book down and help me please.'

As his grandfather walked in and took his place at the table, Roy and his mother set out the plates and the food and sat down to eat. Roy's father got up and lifted the curtains from the window. 'Let's watch a film while we eat,' he said.

They began to eat. The rice, the spiced lentil soup, the vegetable curry, the baked fish, the delectable mutton stew. As they ate, they looked out of the window where the film had begun to play.

A casket in a horse carriage rolled down the Red Road in Calcutta. Roy lay in it. Only his closed eyes and cotton-wool-stuffed nostrils could be seen. The blast had mangled his face and body beyond recognition. The coroners had to stitch his severed legs to his knees.

'You're all good now, not a mark on your body,' said his mother as she patted him gently on his back. Roy smiled and nodded at her as he took a mouthful of fish and rice.

As the camera panned out, first in top shot and then drifting south for a long shot, they could see thousands, hundreds of thousands, millions of people on both sides of the road. Millions more walked with the carriage. The camera took a 360-degree view. A sea of humanity. Then a series of quick close-ups. Kapo, Colonel Aks and Althea, Marshal Zhukov, Marshal Rokossovsky, Marshal Malinovsky, Marshal Bagramyan, Vasily Zaitsev and his sniper party, General Salman, General Bahadur, Brigadier Maria, Brigadier General Paddy, Colonel Abbas, Colonel Suleiman, Brigadier Banerjea, Major Bhavna, Major Hmar, Admiral Limpdick, Admiral Townsend, Vice-Admiral Choksi, Sitaram, Aurelio, Olga the Whore, Elan and his boatmen, Sloth Bear, Blind Hyena, Marshal Bhodi, Bechamoni, Naren, Raven, Civet Cat, Begum Johnson, Black Panther, Talking Crane, Long-Horned Bird, Bhombol and his friends, Chengiz Khan and his Mongol Army, workers, farmers, shop-keepers, bootleggers, rickshaw pullers, taxi drivers, street hawkers, housewives, porters, wage labourers, students, soldiers, prostitutes, ragpickers, undertakers, journalists, failed and acclaimed poets and writers, theatre actors, pickpockets, lumpen louts, wasters, mad men. It was a grand procession. Posters with Roy's face were everywhere.

Countless ospreys flew over the casket in circles. Soon, Laddie and Hobgoblin led a flypast in their First World War biplanes followed by the F-35s. Loudspeakers dotted the way. They blared the 'Internationale' as the carriage rolled on.

'That's what I call a real send-off,' Roy's father exclaimed as the film cut to another location. A condominium, tastefully done up. It was silent. Laila stood in the open kitchen, trying to fix dinner while Ryan was wiping a vinyl disc clean. An antique-looking turntable lay on a wooden table in front of him. It was gleaming. 'He got it fixed,' Roy screamed out in joy. He had put the turntable in the olive bag that he had handed Ryan over.

In front of Laila, on the kitchen counter, lay a handwritten note. Roy recognized Kapo's handwriting. He could read only the last few lines, because a little red book—*The New Pocket World Atlas*—covered the rest: 'He was always recklessly bold, at times verging on the rash. But that was him. No one knows that better than you. He died the way he lived. It was sudden, instant. He did not suffer any pain. We found three things on him. I presume he always carried them on his person. I am sending them to you. One, his wallet. Two, his gunmetal cigarette case. Three, *The New Pocket World Atlas*. I am also sending you his ukulele. If you and/or Ryan ever want to come back to Sands and make this your home, the people of this nation will try to make it as special for you as possible. We owe this much to Roy.'

Laila looked at Ryan as she spoke. 'Ryan, you took Dad's manuscript to the publisher. Did they get back to you?'

'Yes, just this morning. They're going to publish. It'll come out next year.'

'He's just like you, Roy,' said Roy's mother, 'Such a fine man. I always knew Laila would be a wonderful mother.'

'He's a much better man than I ever was,' Roy said as he tried to suck the marrow out of a bone.

The camera moved from Laila to Ryan in slow motion. On the way, Roy could see a family photograph of the three of them up on the wall. Marshal Bhodi was right. His picture was on someone's wall after all. The best wall Roy could have asked for. It was Ryan and Laila's wall. His wall.

Ryan put the disc in its slot and brought down the stylus. As the diamond head hit the vinyl surface, Herbie Mann's flute filled the air.

'I'm sleepy. I think I'll go and crash.' Roy left the dining room. He washed his hands, rinsed his mouth and lay down on his bed. He was asleep in no time. In the background, 'Memphis Underground' was still playing on Ryan's turntable.

A few minutes later, his grandfather and father entered the room.

'Shall I wake him up and break the news?' asked the grandfather.

Roy's mother had quietly followed them in. 'The poor boy is sleeping so peacefully after such a long time. You can always tell him when he wakes up.'

'I'm sorry. I just thought he'd be happy to hear it. Anyway, as soon as he is up, he'll dash off to the football field,' said his grandfather with a smile. They were all smiling. Their little boy was back home after so long.

As soon as Roy's body was taken off ice and rolled into the furnace, the hungry fire reached out with its greedy flames for his clothes. When the heavy metal shutter slammed down, the air in Calcutta reverberated with cries of 'Long Live Comrade Firebrand.' Around 350 international media personnel had flown down to cover the state funeral. There were ministers and presidents from other countries who were in attendance as well.

Just as the fire started biting into Roy's flesh, in distant parts of the world, across various continents, the ground began to shake. The dance of the earth was slow to begin with but then the rhythm picked up before reaching a frenzy. It started from the haplessly poor mining kleptocracies of northwest Africa and quickly cut across the Saharan desert to reach the other end at Somalia where guns are easier to find than bread. From the gold mines in the Peruvian Amazon where thousands of child workers are battling appalling health and safety standards to the adult holiday resorts in Costa Rica where young women are paraded as desserts after drinks and dinner. From the Gadchiroli forests in India where security forces kill, rape and maim the local tribals at will to the Rakhine province of Myanmar where Rohingya Muslims have been massacred to make space for the violent reincarnation of the Buddha. From the American Indian reservations in North America where alcohol and tobacco fill up more than half of the stores' shelves to the Aboriginal lands in Australia. And so many more that you or I could have never kept count of. As the tremors continued, the landmasses began to tear away and float into the seas and oceans, before starting to gravitate towards the Island of Bald Mountain.

Continents were being reshaped. A new one was emerging. The outlines of the maps on General Firebrand's red atlas were becoming irrelevant. And while this cataclysmic reordering of the earth was going on, Roy was asleep, clutching a pillow to his side.

'He is missing out on it,' his grandfather whispered, 'The birth of the new world.'

'It doesn't matter,' his mother whispered back, 'All he's ever seen is turbulence. Let him sleep.'

Roy's father put an arm round his father and his wife and walked them out of the room. Pulling the door shut behind him, he said, 'Let him sleep. Sleep makes everything go away.'

Notes on Characters

Konstantin Konstantinovich Rokossovsky was born in Warsaw, Poland, on 21 December 1896. A legendary Soviet commander during the Second World War, he also served as Poland's Defence Minister from 1949 until 1956. Rokossovsky then returned to the Soviet Union, where he lived until his death in 1968. He lies buried at the Kremlin Wall Necropolis in Moscow. Rokossovsky served in the Imperial Russian Army during the First World War. In 1917, he joined the Red Guards and in 1918 the newly formed Red Army. He fought with great distinction during the Russian Civil War of 1917–22. Rokossovsky held senior commands until 1937 when he fell victim to the Great Purge of Stalin, during which he was branded a traitor, imprisoned and tortured. After Soviet failures in the Winter War of 1939–40, Rokossovsky was taken out of prison and reinstated due to an urgent need for experienced officers. Following Germany's invasion of the Soviet Union in June 1941, Rokossovsky played key roles in the defence of Moscow (1941–42) and the counteroffensives at Stalingrad (1942–43) and Kursk (1943). He was instrumental in planning and executing key parts of Operation Bagration (1944)— one of the most decisive Red Army successes of the war—for which he was made a Marshal of the Soviet Union.

Vasily Grigoryevich Zaitsev, born on 23 March 1915 in Yeleninskoye, Orenburg Governorate, Russia, was a Hero of the Soviet Union and a celebrated Soviet sniper of the Second World War who is famous for developing his technique of the 'sixes' which is used by nearly all militaries today. Between 22 September 1942 and 17 December 1942, Zaitsev registered 265 official enemy kills, 225 of them in the Battle of Stalingrad alone. He was injured and almost lost his eyesight before it was restored by famous ophthalmologist Vladimir Filatov. Zaitsev returned to the front and saw his final action at the Battle of the Seelow Heights as part of the Berlin Offensive in April 1945. Upon retirement, he settled in Kiev, where he died on 15 December 1991, just 11 days before the dissolution of the Soviet Union. He was buried in Kiev though he had wished to be buried in Stalingrad. On 31 January 2006, Vasily Zaitsev was reburied with full military honours at the Stalingrad memorial at Mamayev Kurgan in Stalingrad, present-day Volgograd, Russia.

Lyudmila Mikhailovna Pavlichenko, born on 12 July 1916 in Bila Tserkava, Kiev Oblast, then Russian Empire, was a legendary Soviet sniper in the Red Army during the Second World War. Nicknamed Lady Death, she is credited with killing 309 enemy combatants. She served in the Red Army during the siege of Odessa and the siege of Sevastopol, during the early stages of the fighting on the Eastern Front. Her score of 309 kills probably places her within the top five snipers of all time but most experts say that her kills are likely more numerous. After the war, she became a historian and died in Moscow on 10 October 1974. She lies buried in the Novodevichy Cemetery in the Russian capital. Once, during a tour in the United States, when a journalist mentioned that she had killed a lot of men, she replied: 'Men, not one. Nazis, yes. At least 309 of them.'

Roza Shanina, born on 3 April 1924 in the Russian village of Edma, Arkhangelsk Oblast, was a Soviet sniper in the Second World War credited with over 50 confirmed Nazi kills. On 27 January 1945,

Roza, who named after the Marxist revolutionary Rosa Luxemberg, died in combat during the East Prussian Offensive; her chest was torn apart by a shell fragment. Three of her brothers died in the war. A recipient of the Order of Glory, she lies buried in Znamensk, Kaliningrad Oblast, Russia.

Marshal Bhodi is a fictional character in the Choktar and Fyataru series of stories and novels by cult Bengali writer Nabarun Bhattacharya, my father. His other characters who feature in this novel are Naren, Bechamoni, Raven or Dondobayosh, Civet Cat or Bonberal and Begum Johnson. My father could not finish his last novel, *Mobloge Novel* (A Novel for The Mob) owing to his illness that saw him breathe his last in 2014. The Bengali publishing house that published it left 20 blank pages at the end of the book for the readers to draw their own conclusions. I have used some characters from that novel here. I guess I wanted to give them a sense of closure. I thought I owed it to my old man.

Indra Lal Roy, born on 2 December 1898 in Calcutta, India, was the sole Indian flying ace of the First World War. While serving in the Royal Flying Corps and its successor, the Royal Air Force, he claimed 10 aerial victories over the German Luftwaffe in just over 170 hours of flying time. On 22 July 1918, at the age of 19, Roy or Laddie, as he was called by his colleagues, was shot down over Carvin, France. A Distinguished Flying Cross awardee, he lies buried at Pas De Calais, France. His nephew Subroto Mukerjee served as a fighter pilot in the Second World War and later became the first Indian Chief of Air Staff.

Sardar Hardit Singh Malik, born on 23 November 1894 in Rawalpindi, British India, was an officer in the Royal Flying Corps who was credited with two aerial victories, though he claimed six, which would have made him the only other Indian flying ace of the First World War besides Indra Lal Roy. Of the four Indians who flew with the RFC and RAF during the First World War, Malik was one of the two survivors; the other was Erroll Chunder Sen, who had been a German prisoner of war during 1917–18. He later became a diplomat and was the Indian High Commissioner to Canada and the Indian Ambassador to France. Malik breathed his last on 31 October 1985 in New Delhi. His autobiography, *A Little Work, a Little Play*, was published in 2011.

Georgy Konstantinovich Zhukov, born on 1 December 1896 in Strelkovka (now named Zhukov after him), Kaluga, Russia, was a Marshal of the Soviet Union. He also served as Chief of the General Staff, Minister of Defence, and was a member of the Presidium of the Communist Party (later Politburo). During the Second World War, Zhukov oversaw some of the Red Army's most decisive victories. He organized the defence of Leningrad, Moscow and Stalingrad. He participated in planning several major offensives, including the Battle of Kursk and Operation Bagration. In 1945, Zhukov commanded the 1st Belorussian Front, took part in the Vistula–Oder Offensive and the Battle of Berlin which resulted in the defeat of Nazi Germany. In recognition of Zhukov's role in the war, he was chosen to accept the German Instrument of Surrender and inspect the Moscow Victory Parade of 1945. After the war, Zhukov's success and popularity caused Stalin to see him as a potential threat. Stalin stripped him of his positions and relegated him to military commands of little strategic significance. After Stalin's death, he was appointed Defence Minister in 1955 and made a member of the Presidium. In 1957, Zhukov lost favour again and was forced to retire. He never returned to a position of influence and died on 18 June 1974. Zhukov is remembered as one of the greatest Russian and Soviet military leaders of all time, along with Alexander Suvorov, Mikhail Barclay de Tolly and Mikhail Kutuzov. He is buried in the Kremlin Wall Necropolis.

Rodion Yakovlevich Malinovsky, born on 23 November 1898 in the Odessa region of the then Russian Empire, was a Soviet military commander and a Marshal of the Soviet Union. During the Second World War, he took part in several of the Red Army's key victories over Nazi Germany, including the Battle of Stalingrad and the Siege of Budapest. As Minister of Defence of the Soviet Union from 1957 to 1967, Malinovsky oversaw the strengthening of the Soviet Army. He played a crucial role in the Soviet victory at Stalingrad in December 1942 and helped drive German troops out of Ukraine following the Dnieper–Carpathian offensive. He then commanded the Soviet drive into the Balkans, forcing Romania to switch to the Allied side, for which he was made a Marshal of the Soviet Union by Stalin. He further took part in the liberation of Budapest, Vienna and Prague, cementing Soviet military supremacy in Central Europe. After the German surrender in May 1945, Malinovsky was transferred to the Far East, where he oversaw the defeat of the Japanse Kwantung Army during the Soviet invasion of Manchuria. He received the Soviet Union's highest distinction, the title Hero of the Soviet Union. He died on 31 March 1967 in Moscow and is interned in the Kremlin Wall Necropolis.

Ivan Khristoforovich Bagramyan, also known as Hovhannes Khachaturi Baghramyan, was born on 2 December 1897 in Ganja, Azerbaijan, then Russian Empire, was a Soviet military commander and Marshal of the Soviet Union of Armenian origin. During the Second World War, Bagramyan was the second non-Slavic military officer, after Latvian Max Reyter, to become a commander of a front.

He was among several Armenians in the Soviet Army who held the highest proportion of high-ranking officers in the Soviet military during the war. He was the commander of the fabled Operation Kutuzov in the Battle of Kursk which sealed the fate of Nazi Germany on the Eastern Front in the Second World War. He also played key roles in the liberation of Belarus and the Baltics from Nazi clutches. Marshal Bagramyan was awarded numerous Soviet and foreign orders and medals for his service, including two Orders of the Hero of the Soviet Union, seven Orders of Lenin, the Order of the October Revolution, three Orders of the Red Banner, two Orders of Suvorov and the Order of Kutuzov. Among the other commendations he received were the Polish Polonia Restituta twice and the Medal for the Victory over Germany. He was a prolific writer and left behind encyclopaedic works on the Second World War. He died on 21 September 1982 in Moscow and is buried at the Kremlin Wall Necropolis.